For Our Contributors

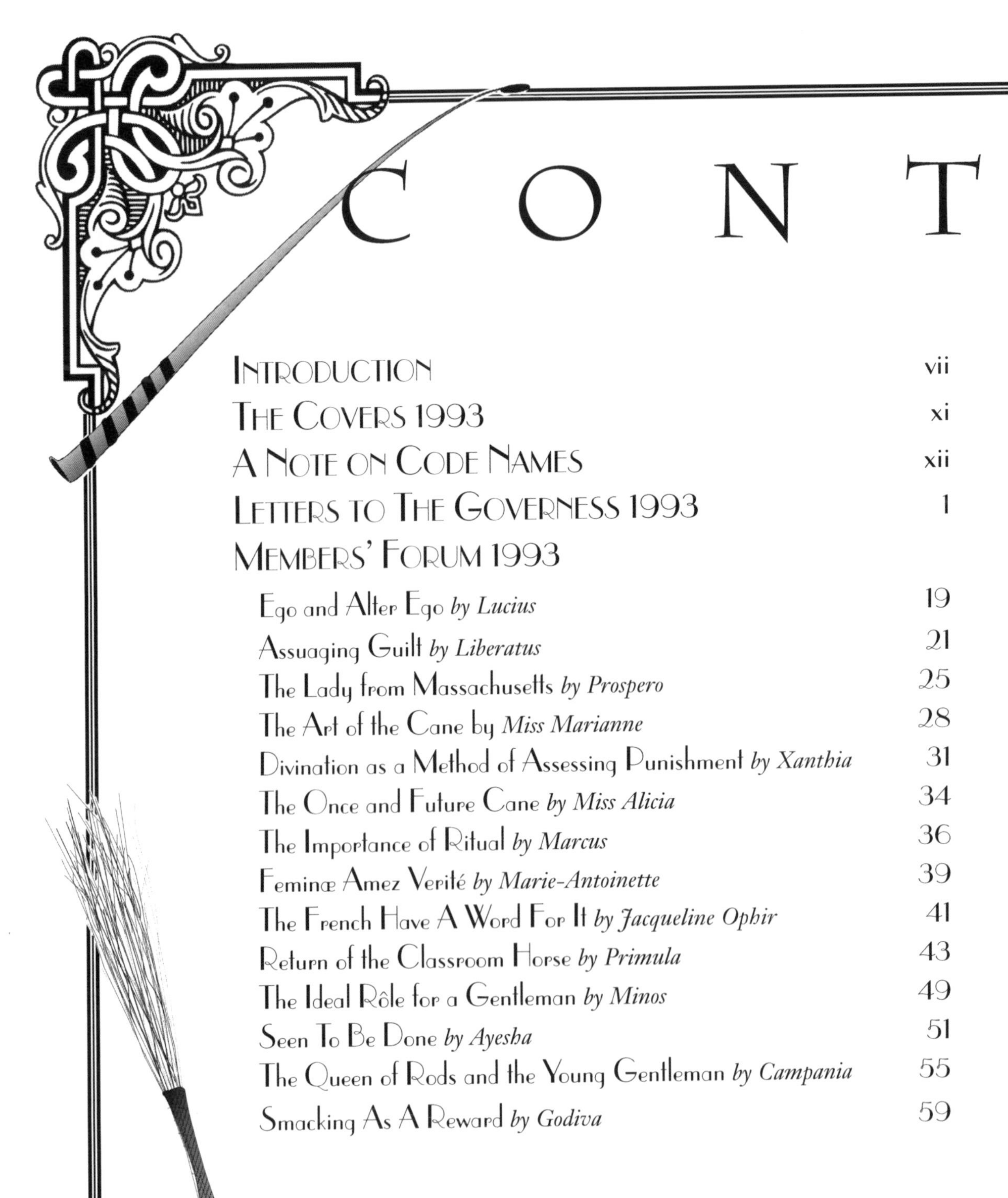

CONT

ENTS

GENERAL FEATURES, BOOK REVIEWS, POETRY 1993

MISCELLANIA

INTRODUCTION

IT IS ALWAYS A PLEASURE to introduce a new book by The Alice Kerr-Sutherland Society. In this case the pleasure is made all the keener by the knowledge that, in presenting *The Governess Compendium* for the delectation (we hope) of readers everywhere, we are also efficiently rescuing ourselves from the consequences of a miscalculation which, from the origins of the Society and *The Governess* itself, has been as annoying as it has been consistent. That is, our longstanding failure to print a sufficiency of Back Issues.

Obviously one does not create Back Issues as such. Back Issues were after all once simply Issues. The appearance of a newer Issue automatically transforms those copies of preceding Issues (that happen to linger on in the editorial offices) into Back Issues. Nevertheless unlike some other classes of apparently superseded product, there is (we have found) a near-constant—and constantly-accelerating—demand for Back Issues of *The Governess*; and the larger the Society's Membership grows, the more fierce becomes this demand. It is one we have never (save a few months at the beginning when we had an apparent superfluity of Issue Ones) been able to meet.

We must be fair to ourselves. A print order is judged, albeit with hindsight, to have been rashly over-optimistic when large numbers of unsold copies linger sadly on as the years roll by. To avoid such debâcles the prudent Publisher habitually takes a more cautious view. But here, too, miscalculation can supervene—one may under-specify the print order. Demand outstrips supply and in a wholly new way one has fallen short of one's potential. With a regularly-published Journal such shortfalls can be particularly aggravating, since much of what lies within each Issue may refer to, or have been stimulated by, material in an earlier Issue. Without the latter whole sections of a continuing debate may be excised from a particular reader's consciousness.

Our excuse for this failure is that from the first we grossly underestimated the attraction *The Governess* would prove to have for *cognoscenti* of Romantic Discipline everywhere (though on another level it naturally delighted us). The Society, and *The Governess*, began life almost on a whimsical basis. We had the inclination, the archives, access to the technology—why not? What we did not have was a superabundance of funds, and so—necessarily—our print orders were modest, not to say conservative; and we were caught out by our own success. Over and over again.

The Governess Compendium is an attempt, not only to rectify the under-provision of earlier Issues (specifically for the benefit of Members of The Society who have joined in recent months and have not been able to acquire Issues One to Four in any form), but also to show, in a single publication, and particularly for those Readers who may not (yet) hold Membership in our Society, what our first year of publication was really like. It contains all—or, more specifically, nearly all—of what was published in Issues One to Four of *The Governess:* Spring, Summer, Autumn and Winter 1993. This was a period in which the Journal was created, changed printers twice, grew in size (from 36 to 56 pages), tried out some ideas which failed to survive (the Competition, the Crossword, the Gallery), and launched others which most decidedly did so (Sardax covers, Members' Forum, From the Archives, *The House in St. John's Wood* serial). Our general interest features of all types especially revealed our contributing Membership as a reservoir of literary and illustrative talent, and, from the very first, their efforts put most other "disciplinary" publications to rout. As a reviewer recently (and generously) said: "It is wholly apparent that the publishers of this delightful little magazine have complete and specialised mastery of their subject."*

For those new to our publications we must explain that *The Governess*

*David Argyle, *ZeitGeist*, Issue 6.

is written by its Membership, though it is also true to say that an "inner phalanx" of long-term Members (including some of the editorial committee) contributes on a regular, or at least semi-regular, basis. Essays, stories and articles are not "bought on" from outside; nor are they accepted from non-Members. The only rule is that one must be a Member to contribute; after that it is a question of the merits of the contribution itself. The efficiency of this policy, and the excellence of the contributions, may be judged from a reading of the book you now hold.

Though it is called a compendium, it is more strictly an anthology, since in strict truth not everything that was to be found in Issues One to Four is here re-published. The most notable absentee is *The House in St. John's Wood*, whose first four episodes (as I write this the last-ever episode is in the process of being composed) of course were published during this period. Those who have faithfully followed the serial, either from its beginnings or at whatever point they commenced their readership of *The Governess*, will be (we hope) relieved to learn that the completed novel will be published in the first half of 1995 as a separate entity.

Also missing are a few minor editorial experiments like the Crosswords and the Competition in Issue One; the former were judged universally to be a failure and were removed by executive fiat after Issue Three; and since our only attempt at a Competition (Issue One) attracted no entries at all (we later repeated, in Issue Five, the technical coup which was most of its *raison d'être*), we also decided to leave that quietly buried.

If anything else is missing, please believe it was not our intention.

We have entirely re-designed—in a larger format than the originals—re-typeset and re-illustrated the original articles, essays, stories, poems and vignettes. Partly to compensate for the few unimportant bits of Issues One to Four that are not present, we have greatly increased (and we think improved) some of the illustrative material. In particular, we have augmented the very popular feature on Louis Malteste (pp. 82–88). We have dated individual items if the chronology is in some way important—for example, Letters and Members' Forum, where in several cases essays or correspondence is in response to something published at an earlier date—but not where it is irrelevant.

Re-reading these works in a body, we were ourselves greatly impressed by the way a "tone of voice" seemed to arrive out of the ether from the very first moment, a tacitly-accepted refinement of phraseology and terminology which has always subsequently harmonised perfectly with our visual style—playful at the beginning, grown (we think) steadily more conservative. Otherwise *The Governess* today is only a slightly different animal to the one represented between these covers. More pages, glossier, better produced—but not, we think, better written. We are above all a Literary Society and the promulgation of excellence in Disciplinary Literature is our chief reason for existence. We believe we have succeeded so far; and we hope that, after reading *The Governess Compendium*, you will agree.

JACQUELINE OPHIR

Editor, The Governess
November 1994

Please note that the Alice Kerr Sutherland Society ceased to exist in 2000.

THE COVERS, 1993

Premier Issue 36 pages, imperfectly printed, and some technical experiments that didn't quite work. It was a start.

Issue 2 increased pages to 44 and featured Louis Malteste on the cover to "trail" the feature inside. It was considerably better.

Issue 3 was larger again—48 pages—and inaugurated our (continuing) tradition of cover art by Sardax. It was the best yet.

At 56 pages, **Issue 4** set a new benchmark for size and quality, and also contained our 1993 Survey on the Disciplinary Female.

A NOTE ON PEN-NAMES

MANY OF THOSE who read—and, we hope, enjoy—*The Governess Compendium* will not (yet) be Members of The Alice Kerr-Sutherland Society, and as a result may be puzzled by the strange names used by our authors and contributors. One notable feature of the Society's conduct of affairs is that it is not a social organisation of any kind. Indeed the opposite is true: great value is set on personal discretion, and all new Members are offered code-names, which of course also become pen-names where literary matters are involved. These names convey absolutely no information (other than gender) about their owners, leaving readers and other Members to draw their own conclusions from careful perusal of the work itself, not to mention their own deductive skills. Which is quite as it should be.

LETTERS
to
'The Governess'

ISSUE 1

Why I Take Issue With Miss Kerr-Sutherland

"Indecorum" and "Immodesty" Criticised by Doyenne Governess

I AM A VICTORIAN Governess and one of my pupils rather tentatively gave me Miss Kerr-Sutherland's book to read. I say "tentatively" because my pupil knows and understands that I countenance nothing written or published after the Year of Our Lord 1959 and the final death of Civilisation. However this book, though indeed a late publication, was, I understand, written some fifty years ago and therefore does not qualify for my ban. In any case I found *A Guide to the Correction of Young Gentlemen* both acceptable and very interesting.

I firmly believe that tension, guilt and general cloudiness of the psyche are dispelled and purified by a good firm punishment and in the book I found plenty of evidence to suggest that Miss Kerr-Sutherland also believes that punishment is cleansing. In this matter we are in harmony.

However I should like to register my disapproval of certain aspects of the administration of punishment as described by Miss Kerr-Sutherland.

On page 51 she refers to the Governess spanking a culprit while he is "squalling and writhing across her elegant lap." No lap is elegant when that sort of nonsense is going on. I'm afraid that none of my pupils—female or male—is allowed the leeway to behave

Miss Kerr-Sutherland: an undue emphasis on shame?

Drawing by CURTUS

badly. There may be the odd occasion when it is appropriate (in order to encourage a necessary softening of the heart) to allow whimpering or tears, but writhing and squalling—never! Punishments should always be conducted in a dignified—and, yes, elegant—manner. A punishment should be a ritual action and rituals are performed contemplatively and with decorum.

I also take issue with the baring of bottoms and the undue emphasis on shame. Bottoms may perhaps legitimately be bared by mothers or nannies of genuine children. Once a "child" is adult in years it is immodest and indecorous to do so. Bare hand-spankings are not very effective over clothes and grown girls can be punished effectively on the tops of their legs, or even, if they have been particularly naughty, on their knickers. But a grown boy is laid face down on my desk and treated to a slipper on his trousered bottom. I find this perfectly acceptable and completely effective.

A punishment should produce the correct degree of remorse in itself and I cannot approve of the ridiculous device of dressing a boy as a girl in order to increase shame. One can see from the trousered and hideous examples of the female sex that infest every street and home in the modern world that cross-dressing produces a confused, deracinated and barren individual.

Boys should understand that softness of heart, generosity of spirit and kindness are noble qualities available to both sexes and they should not be made to feel that vulnerability and softness can only be achieved by a strange and unnatural action.

I do take great exception to these immodest matters but did, I should emphasise, find much of value and interest in the book as a whole.

Miss Marianne

A Contrary View

All women should learn to appreciate—if they do not already do so—the huge symbolic importance of his breeches to the male.

There is no equivalent female garment whose enforced loss or divestiture causes such distress.

Females, of course, wear the same mode of clothing all their lives, but males begin life dressed as females. "Breeching" comes with the transition from infancy to childhood (though in Victorian times it was often delayed well beyond that point), and in many societies has been marked by small celebrations. It was, and remains, a rite of passage.

To lose the prized garment therefore denotes—or brings about—a reversal of this transition, a devastating loss of status. No matter what his real age is, by removing a male's trousers as a necessary part of a corporal punishment—or even as a penalty in its own right—you are instantly and catastrophically reducing him to the age he was when he said farewell to the frocks of his infancy—or thought he had.

Candida

Femininity Hath Its Privileges

Alice Kerr-Sutherland's seminal work *A Guide to the Correction of Young Gentlemen* lucidly emphasises the need for corporal punishment in disciplining boys. She also argues that a different approach should be taken to disciplining boys and girls.

The contrasting approaches to discipline are particularly apparent in those situations where boys and girls are together, such as in a

A 19th-century Dame School, where boys and girls were educated (and dealt with) on exactly similar lines—note the two pupils on the "shame bench" and the (rather heavy-duty) birch-rod on the table.

household where a governess has responsibility for the instruction and welfare of both. In such "co-educational" environments, it is important that the different approaches to disciplining young gentlemen and young ladies are made clear, as they will exercise an important psychological influence.

In the classroom it is vital that boys are addressed by their surnames, whereas girls should be addressed by their first names. Boys should be required to stand up when the Governess enters the room, until they are commanded to sit. Girls, by contrast, should simply be required to sit up straight at their desks.

Most importantly, boys only should be liable to receive corporal punishment. The maximum form of discipline for a girl is a reprimand, accompanied perhaps by an imposition or a detention. The cane however should be used on boys. Disobedient boys should be caned either in private or in public, in front of all other pupils, both male and female. A disobedient boy can receive a public warning from the governess that he will be caned later in private, or if the offence is serious, in public. Public canings should be administered on the seat of the trousers and the miscreant should be positioned so that his seat is facing the other pupils when he bends over. This discrimination is a useful means of improving their discipline, and of creating the correct attitude that should exist between boys and girls.

MARCUS

➢ *In our view Marcus deserves credit for his sense of chivalry—but is such gallantry (or inequity) really justified? We have known many young ladies who would prefer to be treated in the same way as the stronger sex—no more, no less.*

A Suggested Caning Procedure

In order to maximise the effect of a caning the following procedure is suggested, which gradually increases both the pain of the punishment and the attendant humiliation.

Firstly, the young gentleman should be ordered to present himself properly dressed in pullover and shirt and wearing short trousers. He will then have his hands tied together in front of his body in order to prevent him rubbing his bottom. Secondly, a supple cane of medium weight should be selected. The Governess will then inform the boy that he will receive twelve strokes with increasing severity.

The order to bend over for punishment is then given. The Governess will deliver four strokes across the seat of the trousers, pausing after each stroke to allow the full impact to be appreciated. The boy is then ordered to stand and is left in that position for fifteen minutes.

After fifteen minutes the Governess will unfasten the boy's trousers and allow them to fall to his ankles. His shirt is tucked well up his back out of the way. He is ordered to bend over again and four more strokes of the cane are delivered across his underpants. Again he is left standing for fifteen minutes.

Finally the Governess will draw down the boy's underpants and deliver the final four strokes, leaving him for a further fifteen minutes with his bottom displaying the weals left by the cane.

Montjoie

➢ *This procedure certainly extracts the maximum drama from a simple punishment, and there is clearly a place for such ritualisation. But what if the Governess is in a hurry, or if a class is waiting? What do other Governesses think?*

ISSUE 2

An Answer to Miss Marianne

If Discipline is to be effective it must be remembered. Pain, no matter how heavy, is soon forgotten after the event—this is Nature's way. Shame, however, is not so easily forgotten. As the years roll by embarrassing moments are recalled with clarity, with a renewal of the embarrassment. Hence the display of parts of the body not normally on shew heightens the sense of occasion and prevents the event being easily forgotten.

The denuding of those parts to which discipline is to be applied also has practical reasons. It extends the range of effective implements (some are just not practical over clothes). The corrector can more easily see the effect of the strokes and adjust accordingly. The initial "sting" is the most important part of the discipline and only in the most serious cases should deep bruising result. This "sting" is only possible on the bare skin as even a thin layer of material will dull the effect.

Corporal discipline can be of benefit to most people. It was widely used (and still is occasionally, I believe) in religious spiritual training and is a clean, simple remedy for a troubled spirit. It is the greatest pity that today's society rules it out of order.

Donatus

➢ *The essential principle is surely that each Governess must observe rules and procedures with which she personally feels comfortable—and which she regards as proper. Miss Kerr-Sutherland's view was closer to your own than "Miss Marianne's", but there is, and has always been, room for divergence on this and other matters of technique. A Governess whose primary "wand of office" is a supple school cane is not obliged to unbreech culprits for her discipline to be effective. Indeed, by not doing so she reserves this operation as a further sanction, thereby adding refinement to her régime.*

The Ministry of Discipline?

I HAVE JUST completed reading *The Female Disciplinary Manual* published by Imperial Press. They are, I believe, the same people who publish *The Romantic* and who are dedicated to the concept that time should stand still and remain in the 1920s and 1930s, an age when certain values were held in high regard and discipline was accepted as a necessary adjunct to the maintenance of a civilised Society. I believe also that "Miss Marianne", who contributed the article Why I take issue with Miss Kerr-Sutherland, in your first and excellent new publication *The Governess*, represents this same group of people.

I must first applaud the excellent quality of *The Female Disciplinary Manual* and the sentiments and philosophy it expounds. If only we could recreate the conditions of those times and bring about a return to corporal punishment in home and school, allied to a proper respect for authority, then little of the nonsense of young tearaways stealing cars—not to mention the tragic murder of little James Bulger—would occur. The Police and Courts would have a clear mandate to deal effectively with these young thugs, and life would be safer for all of us.

I am also firmly of the belief that this whole matter of discipline and the necessary levels of severity should be placed in the hands of a woman and an advisory team selected by her from like-minded ladies. This new appointment, at Ministerial level, would have wide-ranging powers to direct the decisions of the Courts and impose minimum requirements of disciplinary action in schools and other institutions, both private and State-controlled.

A manual, similar to the one mentioned above, would provide firm guidelines for those entrusted with the task of establishing and executing the necessary levels of discipline and punishment insisted upon.

They would of course, by the same token, provide checks and safeguards to protect culprits from abuse and excesses, whilst applying the necessary degree of severity to provide real and lasting deterrents to would-be miscreants. Misguided "do-gooders" would have no influence in the new order of things.

Turning from the general to the particular, I am afraid I do not agree wholly with Miss Marianne's obviously strongly-held beliefs. Is it not a question of the sensitive Mistress fitting not only the punishment to the crime, but also to the recipient of correction?

Some offenders are more sensitive than others, some have tougher hides. Surely, for the punishment to be lasting and effective, many factors should be taken into account when deciding on the exact level of punishment. The ritual removal of the last shreds of physical protection and modesty must have a profound psychological effect on some, particularly if this is carried out in public (which some formal punishments must necessarily be). However since this must remain the ultimate sanction it should not be for general use.

In addition, since a formal thrashing on "the bare" is of necessity a serious, severe and extremely painful event, isn't it important that the administrator should be able to observe closely the effects of the chastisements and so ensure that the punishment does not become excessively damaging (or too lenient) to create the correct level of retribution intended?

As for "cross dressing", here I agree with Miss Marianne. I can see no benefit from this practice. If it is considered important to introduce an element of shame into the proceedings, there are many other ways to achieve this. Dressing up in female clothes would appear to be aimed at an entirely different and more perverse objective.

However, notwithstanding these minor differences of emphasis, there are now two first-class works of reference in the *Guide* and the *Manual*, for those who would, in an ideal world, be charged with the responsibility of reintroducing decent civilised standards of morality and a sense of self-discipline and responsibility in the younger generation.

Unfortunately I do not think we will be able to turn the clock back—the concept that rights transcend responsibility is now too deeply rooted. So we can only dream of a better and safer world brought about by a return to the old beliefs of Miss Kerr-Sutherland et al. and her sensible application of firm discipline and severe but fair corporal punishment.

Your new publication *The Governess* is an excellent start. I particularly liked the serial *The House in St. John's Wood*, also your practical instructions on the making of birch rods. It was well printed and presented, the prose of the text compact and educated.

The real test is yet to come, of course. Can you maintain the standard and increase the participation of Members and their contributions—as well as finding ever more archive material of a genuine and believable nature? Regrettably there is no contemporary experience of corporal punishment to draw on. Well done, though, and please keep up the good work.

Equus

➢ *"Cross-dressing" (as some call it) is a subject on which views differ sharply. In the opinion of the Editor (which she does not wish to force upon anybody else) the term is less accurate than "Petticoating" in any disciplinary context, and indeed such punishments have a considerable pedigree (as far back as Græco-Roman times). There are certainly objections to it: a (modern) feminist might argue, for once not without justification, that to dress a youth in female clothing with the object of shaming him is a wholesale insult to women.*

The point surely is—is it or is it not a punishment? Two years ago a female teacher in a Hampshire school was "disciplined" (i.e. rebuked) for inflicting this penalty on two junior boys who persistently invaded the girls' toilets. There can be no doubt that the culprits considered it a punishment, which may, after all, provide at least some of the answer.

The notion that the official administration of physical discipline should be under the ægis of a woman is probably the only way that it could ever come about, since men are these days frequently assumed to advocate such procedures solely for sexually-perverse reasons.

Archive Idea

Thank you for the new journal, which I found lively and entertaining. I congratulate you on the contents and the quality of production

I wonder if you would have a corner for a little feature on "Notable Literary Punishments"? The idea would be to draw attention to spankings or canings from the works of certain authors (perhaps one item per issue, in a couple of paragraphs). I can think of a few incidents that may not be known to everyone, and no doubt there are plenty such to choose from:

➢ Roald Dahl writing disapprovingly of his teacher who caned very deliberately, very slowly, taking plenty of time between strokes to light his pipe.

➢ Shelley's tutor thrashing him on the beach, when they were wet from the sea.

➢ A recent novel, Hop Quad Dolly, about an ancient and weird public school, which includes a beating administered with their heavyweight Sultan-of-Molucca cane.

➢ Reminiscences of Dr Temple as a very strict headmaster, before he became Archbishop and so came to crown the Queen.

LUCIUS

➢ *The idea for a literary (both biographical and fictional) archive such as you describe has been with us since the inception of the Society, and readers will find one or two examples in this issue.*

To touch upon your other suggestions in order: (1) the late Roald Dahl, whatever his other talents—and these were considerable—was a fierce opponent of corporal punishment and readers should not expect to find much that chimes with their views in his short novel Boy to which Lucius refers.

To give one example: he and other boys were caned at the instigation of a sweet-shop owner, and in her presence. His (Norwegian) mother saw the marks (she also saw nothing wrong in parading these in front of the boy's sisters), complained to the Headmaster, and removed her son from the school. Plus ça change…

(2) The Shelley episode is mirrored in Swinburne's novel Lesbia Brandon, *to which we shall be referring in future issues.*

(3) Malacca (or Molucca) canes are far too heavy for the infliction of traditional corporal punishment.

(4) Surely it is Dr. Geoffrey Fisher, *Archbishop of Canterbury at the time of the 1952 Coronation and former Headmaster of Repton (1914–1932), to whom you refer? It is a curious reflection on the confused values of our times that our Gracious Queen was crowned at the hands of the most feared disciplinarian of his generation.*

ISSUE 3

Is The Birch's Reputation Justified?

I KNOW THE Society commemorates the Golden Years of Discipline, 1870–1939, and that the birch was a common instrument of punishment in many institutions during that period.

Possibly because my introduction to the subject came later, I have never understood the mystique of the birch. It seems complicated, expensive, difficult to prepare and to keep fresh, short-lived in use and liable to scatter twigs all over the disciplinarian's study or classroom. I doubt whether many ladies know properly how to use it, and they may also be inhibited by their sense of propriety in that it is believed necessary to administer it only on the male malefactor's bare behind.

Miss Kerr-Sutherland in her famous work extolled the birch's virtues in Olympian and Classic terms. In her Pantheon it was reserved for near-ceremonial correction of the most serious of her pupils' faults. Do any Society Members share her view and if so might they be permitted space in *The Governess* to enlighten any sceptics including myself? There are obviously advantages both to the Disciplinarian and to the Disciplined which could beneficially be explained.

CERDIC

➢ *We make no secret that we share Miss Kerr-Sutherland's opinion of this instrument and its proper place in the Disciplinary scheme of things, but ours is not the only view and we endorse Cerdic's call for original or explanatory contributions on this issue. Certainly some of the points he raises might be seen as valid objections. However we cannot forebear to answer some them ourselves: The birch is complicated and difficult to prepare, certainly (the same might be said of any culinary masterpiece worth the eating, or any book worth the writing, in short for any useful or desirable entity) but expensive? Birch is entirely free, a renewable resource that is common all over the British Isles and other parts of the Northern Hemisphere. We must agree that it is both difficult to keep fresh and short-lived in use (if used properly), but the objection to the débris of twig-ends can surely be met by setting the recently punished culprit to the task of gathering these up before quitting the punishment chamber. The subject of bare bottoms is another topic entirely.*

Why We (Still) Take Issue With Marianne

It is my opinion that Miss Marianne shows a lack of understanding of the basic requirements of the application of traditional discipline **[see p. 3]**. An over-the-knee spanking is unique in the sense of abject humiliation and contrition experienced by the recipient.

The command 'let down the trousers and go across my knee, boy', followed by the lowering of pants whilst in position, is as effective in terms of the actual punishment as the actual spanking that follows.

Furthermore an experienced governess would be more than competent in ensuring that a prolonged spanking with the culprit correctly in position and quietly accepting his fate is a most effective punishment, just as efficient as Marianne's slipper but for more exemplary.

It is acknowledged that slipper and cane have their place in the repertoire of any disciplinarian but never underestimate the power and punitive merits of a spanking.

Montana

Surely having to bare one's bottom (or have one's bottom bared) is an essential part of the act which, in itself, takes the delinquent back to his or her childhood.

Concern for the modesty of the guilty party has never played a major part in the application of discipline. The history of the religious houses, monasteries, nunneries and schools where physical discipline ruled reveals that the so-called "Inferior" Discipline was applied to the bare buttocks of both male and female and not infrequently by males to females (and vice versa). And this in an environment where, if anywhere, modesty would, one might surmise, have been a major consideration.

In the history of education Discipline was invariably applied on the bare, and even at the time when table legs were considered indecent, bottoms were bared with little thought for the modesty of the victim, who was often placed in positions which destroyed any vestige of it.

In more recent times I have talked to retired teachers, married and single ladies of the highest moral standards and decency who, had they been so authorised during their time in school, would have taken trousers and knickers down with a fair degree of satisfaction, while the modesty of the unfortunate would have been given a low priority indeed.

To end the modesty aspect I read somewhere of a lady left to bring up a mixed family who claimed: "I strapped them, bare bottomed, on their beds when need be. Neither they nor I ever raised modesty as an excuse."

Moreover, there are important practical aspects to be considered. Baring allows the administrator to judge the ability of the area to accept the intended punishment and to adjust if needed.

It allows her to monitor the bottom; by noting if one area is more affected than another she can make allowances and so spread the punishment equally.

As Miss Marianne also uses the strap and cane she must use additional force to obtain results and cannot gauge any damage she may be causing. As for using a slipper through pants—possibly also vest, shirt-tail and trousers—this seems wasted effort unless she uses the heel which is to be deplored as a bruising agent.

DORIAN

IT IS OF the utmost importance that humiliation and "shame-clothing" be used as part-punishment of the obnoxious male adolescent. To rely on corporal correction alone in the education of the older teenager would necessitate very severe application to have any real effect. With the combination of "shame clothing' and the baring of the breech before chastisement, one may lessen the infliction of the physical punishment in order to get a quicker and better improvement in the miscreant's behaviour. Our Patroness was most specific on this point. I can well imagine the secret smirks on the faces of Marianne's pupils as they receive a slipper across their backsides, cossetted no doubt with a good thick pair of underpants beneath.

CONDE

➢ *Before closing this particular correspondence, we feel obliged to step forward to Miss Marianne's defence, since it was we (Editors) who asked her to "open the batting" on our correspondence pages by deliberately taking issue with those of Miss Kerr-Sutherland's precepts with which we already knew her to be in disagreement. This she did with considerable courage, and a forthrightness entirely typical of her (as all who have the honour of knowing her will testify).*

It is safe to conclude that no issue she might have chosen could have proved so contentious, as the response shews (we have printed only a proportion of letters received). However we must say that we find it interesting that those who argue so fiercely for the type of humiliation she deplored are all of the gender who might most expect to suffer accordingly; and we venture the opinion that to some extent this proves her point.

Discipline, as a subject, may be expected to embrace an entire spectrum of activities, with Refinement at one end and raw Libido at the other. There is room for all, of course; and we would add that here we ourselves do not fully agree with Miss Marianne, adhering more closely to Miss Kerr-Sutherland's views; but we entirely see her point that Discipline in its most refined sense requires neither déculottage *nor petticoating; that the introduction of such motifs and procedures can introduce more sensuality into the punishment than might be appropriate; and that in the last resort it is entirely a matter for the disciplinarienne to decide, in accordance with her own empirical experiences, not to mention tastes and prejudices.*

The Pipe, The Cane and The Archbishop

SURELY ROALD Dahl's Headmaster, who spent time administering to his pipe between applying the ten strokes of a caning, was also Dr. Geoffrey Fisher?

I was assured a few years ago by a retired reverend Headmaster (himself a formidable disciplinarian) that Dahl's description was unreliable since he was never caned at Repton. He must therefore have had to rely on second hand evidence, and schoolboys are notorious for exaggerating the extent and severity of their punishments.

CAMPANIA

➢ *Other readers have made the same observations. Campania's final point—to wit, that boys are prone to wilful exaggeration, not least because it enhances their own heroism—is well taken; and there certainly seems to be some doubt whether or not the youthful Dahl personally underwent the described caning, at the hands of the future Archbishop of Canterbury or anybody else. However we must add that if the story is true (to any extent), then it reflects no credit whatsoever on whoever carried out this punishment in the manner described.*

There are times when pipe-smoking may be permitted, even encouraged, but surely not during the infliction of physical correction. At the very least, it shews a cynical disregard for propriety, it is disrespectful to the canee and it disturbs the sanctity of the event itself. Few female disciplinarians would take their duties so lightly or discharge them in so bizarre a fashion.

The Case For Sparing The Rod

AM I ALONE in detecting a lack of balance in the definition of Discipline apparently espoused by the majority of your correspondents? They equate it with Punishment, when as all practising disciplinarians know, the higher interests of Discipline and Social Order, and certainly those of Justice, are often served by a display of compassion. There are times when a punishment may be merited under the letter of whatever Law is in operation; but when it should be remitted (or reduced) nonetheless because of other factors which no purely codified system can ever take into account. Governesses should beware of rigidity, and not be afraid to spare the rod on occasion.

GALLA PLACIDIA

➢ *We endorse this sound, if infrequently stated, viewpoint—with the proviso that compassion, if overdone or predictable, can easily become weakness—and therefore an enemy of good Discipline.*

ISSUE 4

In Hope of Rescue by the Fair Sex

I HOPE THIS letter will be instructive and enlightening to male readers of this excellent journal and of interest to female disciplinarians. As a man I write in a spirit of self criticism and criticism of the male sex generally. My aim is to make out a case for the benefits to mankind of submitting to the will of dominant women.

To be placed in the care and control of the female sex is the only way that we men can be saved from our inflated egos and aggressive, uncaring tendencies. A more responsible and considerate kind of male is the one thing needful for a better world to live in. I believe Marie Antoinette is correct in exhorting Englishwomen to assert their dominance over "unruly sons and disobedient husbands" **[see page 39]** and if that means on occasion having to bend over for the hand, strap or cane then so be it. To use an oft-quoted cliché: "No pain, no gain."

Clearly there are serious but not I believe insurmountable obstacles to persuading members of the male sex to surrender ourselves to a disciplined lifestyle determined and run by women. As a first stage in the proceedings I would suggest that we men should acknowledge our faults as men.

This would entail a complete re-evaluation of our attitudes towards women and an abandonment of the belief in our own innate superiority. I have often thought that during the marriage ceremony it should be the husband who pledges "obedience" to his intended wife and not the usual demeaning arrangement. This would set the tone of his relationship and would encourage his wife to take up her rightful place as the superior sex.

Men are usually one dimensional. We find it difficult to perceive the world in a generous and open-ended way and are unable to break away from the narrow confines of masculinity. We need the female sex to teach, instruct and train us to see things differently. Given the historical burden of transforming ourselves into reasonable and caring human beings rather than remaining the shallow egotistical creatures that we are, women are the only people to whom we can entrust this great task. We need them to help us to help ourselves.

It would be difficult to begin with. A very strict régime would have to be enforced. Surrendering to training in respect, obedience and humility can be a bitter pill for us to swallow but the end would justify the means.

I feel terribly nervous in making this proposal but it seems to me to be the only way of breaking the ice of masculine obstruction to a more productive and enlightened way of living. I would suggest that we males should willingly submit ourselves, once a month, to a punishment. We should obediently accept whatever our wives, mothers or girlfriends choose to give us. Whether it be a spanking, caning or the birch we should not view this as a vindictive act of revenge or retribution on the part of our patroness and mentor. On the contrary, this should be seen as a means of genuine commitment from us to change ourselves through discipline.

The male behind, of course, is the last refuge of the scoundrel male ego. To have our bottoms bared for punishment goes some considerable way to deflating our overblown view of ourselves. To be partially clothed or completely naked for punishment at the hands of a member of the female sex should be sought with pride not approached with bitterness and resentment. Think of the punishment, even if it hurts, and the removal of clothes as the stripping away of layers of imprisoning masculinity.

This does not mean that we would suffer a loss of self confidence or selfesteem. On the contrary. We would be able to breathe new vigour and meaning into our lives knowing full well that we could trust to the more powerful, loving and superior sex to keep us on the straight and narrow.

OPPIDAM

➢ *We agree wholeheartedly—until we examine random (younger) samples of our own sex, when it often seems to us that there is little, if any, apparent superiority over the male.*

For Once, the Other Cheek

CONGRATULATIONS ON the third issue of *The Governess;* a charming collection of previously published work, new material, members' letters and critiques.

There is one matter however on which I have to disagree. Spanking does not make one ashamed. If I have done something of which my Mistress (although I have not been fortunate enough to have had one for some years) strongly disapproves, I know that retribution will follow. There is nothing more shameful in having to lie across my Mistress's lap and be spanked than there is is being secured to a frame and whipped. What I have always found shaming, indeed really humiliating, is to be slapped across the face. It may be that, being a gentlewoman, you feel that slapping the face is the act of a common person and therefore not for you but let me assure you that most men can be quickly brought to heel by such methods, especially if applied in public.

I am sorry to disagree, but I feel sure that other male Associate Members would agree with me.

PRACTICUS

I WOULD LIKE to congratulate you on an excellent and stylish publication. Nevertheless I notice that in the two issues which I have read, there is no reference to punishment on the hands. I know that some consider punishment of this sort unæsthetic, and also possibly dangerous, but my experience is that it has a valuable place in the armoury of a Governess.

The lady for whom I often perform domestic services has no hesitation in strapping me on the hands if she is in any way dissatisfied with the quality of my work. I find it very painful, and it is a punishment which I strive to avoid, though of course I accept it with a good grace, when it is awarded.

However the technique is important. The punishment strokes should be delivered to the palm of the hand, not the fingers, as the delicate joints can be bruised. For the same reason it is not appropriate to use a hard instrument, particularly a cane. But my lady has a broad leather strap mounted on a wooden handle, which when delivered firmly from over the shoulder causes intense stinging and smarting, and a tingling sensation that can last for quite a long time.

But it has never caused me any bruising or marks, and the hands remain ready for whatever tasks are required. The usual punishment is three strokes on each hand, but as many as six can be awarded in case of more serious faults.

Apart from the intense pain which is caused at the time, there are two reasons why I think this type of punishment is of value. Firstly the method of delivery means that the boy to be punished must face his punisher and see each stroke being delivered on his hand. The self discipline which this requires, and the eye contact with the punisher, in my experience deepens the relationship between the two, and so helps to cement the bond of respect and affection that should always exist between he who is punished, and she who punishes.

Secondly, strapping on the hand can be done quickly, and without the need to adjust clothing or adopt a special position. This is very useful in administering immediate punishment particularly in those more public situations when for reasons of decency, or for fear of embarrassing the onlookers, the removal of clothing is not immediately convenient.

OZYMANDIAS

Recollections of the Repton Rod (Reprise)

CAMPANIA IS QUITE correct **[p.4]** in stating that Roald Dahl himself was never caned at Repton. The author indeed openly acknowledges that it was his best friend Michael who was so punished. Allowing for the possibility of exaggeration, as suggested by Campania, to my mind the story does have a ring of truth about it. This opinion is strengthened by my knowledge that quite severe canings were being administered at Repton even some years after the incident reported by Dahl, and after the departure of the Reverend Dr. Fisher. It appears that something of a tradition of bare bottom caning had developed.

My knowledge of this is derived from a gentleman, some twenty years or so younger than Dahl, who attended this excellent school. The circumstances under which we met would give no reason to suppose that my acquaintance was lying, and our conversation took place before Dahl's book was published.

My acquaintance told me that while a pupil at Repton he had been caught smoking in the school toilets. This was both against the school rules, and in any case illegal for a boy of his age. The punishment meted out for this crime was as follows.

First he was ordered to take down his trousers and underpants. He was then made to bend over and was given twelve hard strokes with the cane across his bare bottom. My acquaintance told me that this was by far the worst beating he had ever received—and incidentally, he never smoked again!

Further interesting light on the history of Repton may be found in the (fictional) works of Aubrey Fowkes, the pseudonym of R. Vere Cripps. Fowkes produced a number of books which contain flagellatory themes and his *New Face at Repton Hall* is a good example. (Fowkes clearly knew Repton and there is a strong possibility that he may even have been educated there.) In this book there are many accounts of canings and birchings. At one point a quote describes the preparation for the birch and how "they fairly soon had him kneeling on the block with his trousers down and his shirt rucked back, and presenting just his sturdy bottom… "

> The twigs seemed to flick the flesh rather than cut it, though inflicting as was plain from the chap's visceral winces and writhings a lively degree of pain, but it looked altogether different from the rather mangling business Francis had seen at his first school—compared with that, when the victim had bellowed like mad, this birching was refined.

18th Century Westminster rather than 20th century Repton but the principle remains the same.

Political cartoon (of Nicholas Udall) by Gillray.

It would seem to me that these works may well be worth examining. For those members who have not visited Repton I can confirm that even today it has the air of a 19th century Public School. It is almost possible to hear the steady "thwack" of rattan across adolescent buttocks or the swish of the birch echoing around the Great Hall, and the sundial, mentioned by Fowkes, is still there with its exhortation engraved in the ancient stone:

Fugit hora, Ora labora.
("Time flies: Pray; Work")

MONTJOIE

➢ *An examination of the works of Fowkes, who combined a strong social conscience with an unparalleled knowledge of Victorian judicial and scholastic punishments—though seldom if ever involving females in either rôle—is planned for a future issue. We understand he was indeed a pupil at Repton.*

FROM THE ARCHIVES

THE ROD

From an 1808 Children's Book

Little George would
not be dress'd
He pouted, scream'd
and cried;
Repuls'd the maid
if she caress'd
And all he
threats defied..

He gave her many a fruitless blow,
To keep off soap and water;
But, at last was made to know
'Twas wrong that he had fought her.

For when the rod
appear'd in sight,
His passion soon
was cool'd,
His face was wash'd,
and all was right
And George was
quickly rul'd.

MEMBERS' FORUM

1993

ISSUE 1

EGO & ALTER EGO

A Voyage into the Subconscious of a Submissive.

By LUCIUS

I AM LUCIUS. You may reasonably judge me very ordinary and boringly middle-aged, but I'm aware of being somehow different. You see, I have these two other complicated fellows always active and milling in my mind. Their adventures are more real than any dull experience of mine. Are they just facets of my personality, or do they lead their own real lives, breaking out from the confines of my unexciting body? You must judge for yourselves, by joining the voyeurs' viewing gallery and witnessing these two experiences that highlighted my week...

Today you see the laid-back me, L. Jekyll, hedonist, reclining happily naked on the massage couch. Jekyll is totally addicted to this sybaritic luxury, cannot survive the week without a generous fix of luxurious relaxation.

Tomorrow, come and inspect that other me, the notoriously naughty Lucius Hyde; once he ruled over others but now that he's disempowered himself, he venerates the powerful. Hyde is a hedonist of quite another kind. Him you will shortly see on quaking knees before the punishment block, secretly relishing his dangerous rendezvous with an implacable mistress.

Jekyll's massage must be long and exquisitely languorous, to the accompaniment of exotic fragrances and soothing music, an orchestrated voyage into contentment. I bare my body—this is L. J. speaking—to a motherly masseuse, my angel come to earth, with genius in her ministering hands, which probe into my mind as well as into every crevice of my body. Knots are unknotted, tensions released, and my holistic soul refreshed. Buttocks are pummelled deeply, cossetted, cherished, sweetly stroked, until my inner self regresses into blessed infancy (in Jekyll's childhood perhaps, or is it Hyde's?).

Thus is my body pampered and prepared to play tomorrow's rôle as the offending Hyde, who's born to sin and suffer. Observe the spectacle of the stark punishment room, and hear its dramatic sounds. No languor here. For this offending male the penalty can only be short, sharp and shocking. A vigorous and threatening step announces the arrival of Madame, who will preside. She loses not a moment. One devastating look, one commanding gesture, and the penitent's trousers crumple around his ankles. Pants fall below his knees, exposing his plump buttocks. In silent ritual he bends down across the block, baring his elevated bottom skywards. (Viewers, you see a handsome pair of globes, fleshy and pale, designed by Nature to be the perfect seat for all necessary, serious, corrective discipline. Those pallid surfaces are offered as a sacrifice to the Lady Dominant, and will not be refused.)

Yes, Ma'am. The fault was mine. I do confess. Madame, aloof, thoughtfully flexes the slender cane in her capable hands. Confession comes too late, when the offence is brazenly repeated. I shall apply one dozen strokes. Remain quite still. Count each one out, and very loudly.

Suspense is palpable. The mind tingles, sharply tuned in, to an excruciating frequency. This is the high noon of expectancy, a moment waiting to explode. Watch Hyde take a gasping breath, then…

THWACKKKK!!!

I howl inside—yes, I am there, in the flesh, and never yet more conscious of my flesh, the object of Madame's focused attention. Ten thousand nerves have shot their scorching signals to the brain. My mind trembles to record an expert's stroke that heralds the overwhelming, searing strokes that still are promised.

THWIPPP!! Aah… My scream is silent, but I count. TWO!

THWACKK!! Ooh… aah… THREE!

CRACKKK!! Ai, ai, ai, ai… FOUR!

Another rushing sound, another stroke. The timing's slow and brilliant. Another, and another. My count is loud but strangulated, my body shivers while my buttocks rise still higher. FIVE! SIX! A longer moment of refined suspense. SEVEN! I feel my buttocks writhe, as pain stabs at the the tenderest site of all. EIGHT! The cane now hotly burns, and flaming arrows reach my brain. NINE! TEN! My bottom's blazing, blazing, blazing, till I groan and swallow down a cry.

ELEVEN! Can this be borne? TWELVE! Oh, blessed twelve, oh bliss. No extra penalties, thanks be!

Madame is speaking. You may stand.

I heave my shaking body up and hear my far-off voice:

I thank you, Ma'am.

Lucius feels the accumulated pain of his full dozen weals, throbbing in one wide ripening stripe across his wobbling buttocks. (Viewers, inspect this proving of the lady's skill.)

But the hot-bottomed penitent is finally at peace. Lucius accepts what he once feared. He thought he hated that supreme sensation, but now he knows he has received the full enlightenment.

He knows, beyond all doubt, just how supremely he appreciated the correction.

Hyde has surrendered (yes, I am he—Jekyll surrendered too). How all of us do surely know that nothing else in our experience can match this painful bliss, this blissful pain.

We thank you, Ma'am, we thank you. ✤

ISSUE 2

ASSUAGING GUILT

The Social Mechanics of Corporal Punishment

By Liberatus

In my youth it was generally accepted that discipline was an essential factor in character development. It was applied caringly, and sometimes even uncaringly, in school and home; and with various methods, from the angry slap to the coldly applied judicial caning. I think that it would be a fair generalisation to assert that the higher the social standing of the family, the more the likelihood of it being the latter and of a cane being in evidence; often to be found openly in view within the walking sticks collected in a typical hallway stand.

It would be wrong to assert a belief that this probability confirms that the use of the cane produced the higher social standing, but it was certainly true that such families placed great store on formality and the value of discipline in developing correctness of behaviour and educational application. Correct behaviour also gave particular emphasis to the giving of respect to others, especially to ladies and those assigned with authority. Those in authority who were ladies, therefore, were expected to apply such discipline as was merited in maintaining their position of respect.

There came a war and war is usually a focus for the force of change. Psychiatrists established a creed that human behaviour was determined environmentally and that heredity was a factor only in so much as it determined the environment. Therefore it was reasoned that, by providing neat new council houses, the social problems of inner city tenements would be cured along with homelessness. It also meant that any behavioural problem could be presumed to result from some defect in the upbringing and that the cure lay in the understanding of the cause, rather than in the discouraging effect of discipline. Egalitarianism in education and opportunity would bring about the ideal society which would encompass freedom of thought and deed; and that encouragement was all powerful in terms of motivation and that the sanction of discipline was positively harmful to character development.

It is strange to reflect that our science has now developed a better understanding of genetics; that the D.N.A. molecule can even transmit genes which determine behaviour. Anyone who had thought about nature already knew this. Dogs, for example, clearly demonstrate behaviour, such as fetching or digging, according to the breed, almost regardless of environment. Could it be that human tendencies to violence or deceit have inherited dimensions and, if so, does this influence the determination of the most effective remedy? Can encouragement of good behaviour be made even more effective in terms of motivation if it is supported by discouragement of bad behaviour? It has also been demonstrated by "Biogenetics" that tactile sensation and the release of suppressed feelings in physical form can have deep psychological effect. Therefore, if the defective behavioural characteristic has any inheritance factor, or is deeply based, then discipline which has physical impact on feelings is more likely to have a deeper and more lasting effect.

One can also consider emotional needs. A poem which expresses my own feelings commences:

> Is it romance or is it lust
> Which binds our needs together
> Or is there something in the blood
> Which is like the lure of leather?

I have to consider it possible that my own interest in discipline has some inherited background. It would be easier to accept if it was simply based on either a submissive or a dominant nature. However, it is surprising that most personalities which exhibit one or other of these characteristics will also exhibit the contrasting one in certain circumstances.

Many people who share such an interest in discipline will be able to relate childhood experiences which seem to confirm that some event determined their nature. Rousseau, in his Confessions, recalls the emotional impact of being chastised by Mlle. Lambercier. It is quite possible that such experiences can give direction to the underlying characteristic, such as submissiveness, particularly if reinforced at puberty to become part of the sensual motivation. However, it is also possible that such people are prone to be more influenced by, and even seek out, such experiences by virtue of some inherent drive.

My own experiences seem to be unusual in that I remember vividly the occasions when I avoided the punishment deserved and was left with very bad feelings of guilt—particularly when others were punished on my account. When other memories become a haze, every little detail of the events remains. They had impact and consequence in terms of self confidence and diminished self respect. How much more creative energy would have been available, and could yet be available, without the need to suppress such feelings? Or are the events irrelevant, being only the focus of a predetermined nature?

A description of the events needs to be set in the context of the age and the environment. I attended an Elementary School which was populated by children from mainly poor homes but, at the age of ten, I was blissfully unaware of concepts of privilege. On reflection, it was a privileged education in that the teaching was rigorous and successful, with two thirds of the children passing the Eleven Plus examination. The staff were mostly female and the Headmistress, Miss Grindley, commanded great respect—and knew how to make her cane effectively known and, occasionally, felt. Just bringing the flexible yellow wand into a classroom was sufficient to ensure perfect order.

One scene, in the playground, is still clear in my mind. I stupidly approached a much bigger boy and, out of bravado, provoked him to fight. I actually believed that my friends would rally round. It was horrifying to find instead that an excited square had formed and that I was in the middle and likely to be hurt. It was fortunate that a teacher appeared and we were marched off to wait outside the study until the Headmistress was able to deal with us. Fighting invariably resulted in a caning and I was extremely frightened; and time seemed everlasting as I contemplated the consequences.

When we were confronted I behaved terribly. I found myself lying about my innocence and the way in which I had been victimised; but the Headmistress simply concluded that she would punish us both with four strokes of the cane. I was first and my caning was a complete anticlimax. I bent over and waited for the pain. None came. The four strokes were so gentle as to be a mere token. The other boy's were not—my lies apparently having been believed. I remember my shame and probably carry it with me even after all these years. Dear Miss Grindley, how I wish that you had been more resolute.

It then amazed everyone that the eleven plus examination found me designated to attend a posh minor public school which only accepted a few scholarship boys. I had never exhibited any tendency to shine but the exam was a form of intelligence test, rather than the three R's which had been so successfully installed into us all. Thereafter my schooldays were not particularly enjoyable, but my education was of a high order and in the company of others whose academic abilities kept my own modestly in perspective.

This school was ruled by the prefects with dramatic use of the cane. The Masters were seldom, if ever, required to act as disciplinarians, they were just able to get on with their teaching function. The prefects wore short gowns and held regular lunchtime prefects' meetings for the purpose of discipline. They were not empowered to deliver more than three strokes of the cane, but they had developed the technique of running in and delivering each one with savage ferocity. Even the bravest was beaten into compliance.

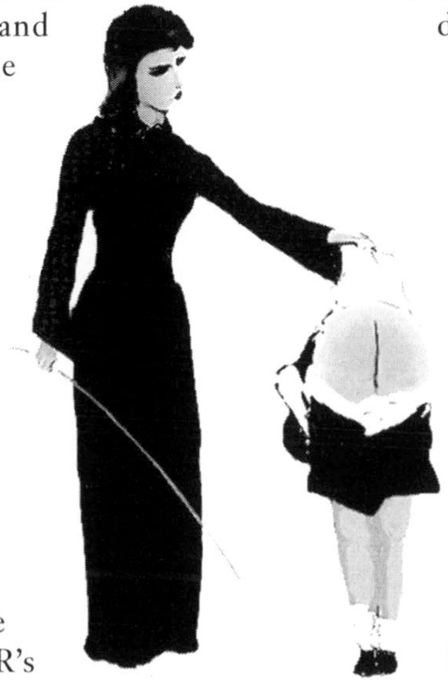

Near the end of my first year I was caught talking in morning assembly and summoned to attend the prefects' meeting at 12 o'clock. The rest of the morning was spent in dreadful expectation and it was even worse having to stand outside the big oak door of the prefect's room, together with seven other miscreants. One by one they were taken in, the door being opened, the name shouted, and the door slammed shut. The victim had to knock and enter and answer to the accusation whilst standing in front of the big table which had a collection of canes arranged carefully in front of him, and the prefects seated formally around the other three sides. He was then sent out to await the verdict. The same entry procedure was repeated but, if he was to be beaten, the canes would no longer be on the table but would be flexing in ready hands.

I waited whilst the formalities were applied to all the others and heard the horrific thwacks as the cane was applied. In fact, the whole school seemed to hush at such moments and people counted as the strokes echoed down the stone corridors. The beaten victims emerged in distress, some putting on a brave face, but mostly it shewed and you lowered your eyes as they shuffled off to the toilets to regain composure.

My own entrance was another anti climax. I was told that my case would be referred to the head of lower school because they needed permission before beating a first year boy—but that this was a formality. Days of fear followed and a prefect entered the classroom to summon a boy to attend that day's prefects' meeting. I knew it was for me and that they had received the appropriate permission. However, the prefect stumbled over the name and excused himself for being unable to decipher the writing. Meanwhile, everyone in the class was looking at me.

So the fear kept on. It was the last week of term and I was not called—so I was thinking about the prospect during the holidays and hated my return. Still I wasn't called and it gradually dawned on me that they were not going to carry out the sentence. So I was always careful until, two years later, I was caught indulging in horseplay prior to a lesson. It was my fault. I had started a mock sword fight with my best friend, who was over a foot taller, and the class enjoyed our antics until the prefect entered.

We were called before the prefects together (the ominous canes before us) and said nothing in our defence before being sent out to await the verdict. I was taken in first and was relieved to see the canes still on the table in front of me. It was explained that, as it was a first offence and as I was such a little chap, that they were dismissing me with a caution as to my future behaviour. Malcolm was then taken in and I was mortified to hear the running steps and the echoing thwacks of a full three-stroke thrashing. He came out devastated and ignored me, and our friendship never recovered. It had been mostly my fault and he was the only one to suffer.

The point of these anecdotes is that the mistaken non-application of deserved discipline can actually do psychological damage. How much better to suffer the pain of the consequences than to be left with a sense of guilt. I will never know to what extent I was damaged by these events or whether they caused my special interest in corporal punishment. I feel that they are significant and that I still have some deep desire to assuage my guilt—to wait in dreadful expectation which does not result in anti climax but in the feeling that, although painful, justice and inner peace comes at last. ✤

➢*There can be few who will have read this analysis unmoved or without a sense of admiration for its honesty and clear thinking. In our view, Liberatus correctly identifies the chief psychic ill that besets modern Society, though corporal punishment, even when obviously "deserved", is not a universal remedy, and there are undoubtedly those for whom its application would be harmful (for a variety of reasons). But no less harmful is the experience of the "naughty" (i.e. explorative) child who deliberately, if subconsciously, provokes physical chastisement—having already made up his mind to endure it—and is then denied the ritual climax of this ancient rite of passage.*

We cannot be so sanguine about the well known (if now extinct) practice of allowing adolescent youths physical disciplinary powers over younger boys. Young ladies may be mature enough at 17 or 18 to be granted such powers over junior pupils, but boys are most decidedly not—witness the contemporary (and wholly unnecessary) practice of "running-in", which Liberatus describes and which was also a fashion at many other public schools (including Eton) of the period. The gloating quality of the "court martial" procedure is also disturbing—even (that much misused word) sadistic. Physical punishment should be a calm and just proceeding, carried out with the good of the recipient (rather than the gratification of the punisher) in mind. The ritualisation of the event is in order to provide a "pace", and also to afford both parties a framework for self-control. Only rarely should Ritual be used to intimidate, and never to oppress. Liberatus is lucky to have come through these experiences in such a sane and unharmed condition.

The Lady From Massachusetts

WHILE THE IMAGE of the woman I so craved had been deep in my heart since early childhood, the ideal setting was brought into focus by the classic novel *Harriet Marwood, Governess.* The intensity, love, and obsession between the governess and her charge was simply perfect, and I had re-read the book several times, wondering if a woman existed in today's world to play the part in fantasy.

"Vanessa" was just that woman, and we met in 1978. That was long before there were hundreds of ads in various periodicals in which to seek like minded adults for fantasy rôle playing. The one source in my area was a weekly newspaper whose personals section, at that time, was a supermarket for esoteric sexual tastes.

Her ad leaped out at me with phrases like "seeking a naughty boy age 18 to 35" and "redden your bottom with skill and understanding." Naturally, the competition was stiff (I later learned she received some 125 responses). Yet my first letter was appealing enough for her to respond, and the letters started from there.

For months it was letters only, not even a phone call, and that only added to the anticipation. It was in my third or so note to her that I asked if she was familiar with Harriet Marwood. When she responded by writing, "My dear boy, I've memorised it!" I was hooked.

I was 30 when we first met at an outdoor café in Harvard Square on a gorgeous June afternoon. I had had no past experience in such adventures, and that naturally led to anxiety as I looked around for her. When I finally spotted her alone at a corner table, her knowing smile made my fears vanish and instead I wondered whatever had I done to be rewarded with such good fortune. She was 35, elegant in appearance, well spoken and very worldly—all the elements I had hoped for. She spoke with just a hint of reserve, yet the underlying firmness of her unique voice was apparent from the start. That voice was so important, as many will understand. We chatted for some 90 minutes that afternoon; I remember she had brought along her own hardcover copy of Harriet. By the time we said goodbye, I was nothing short of enchanted. Her parting words were "pleasant dreams" as if there were any doubt that such would occur. We met twice more that summer (for dinner), and the letters kept flowing in between.

Our début contribution from the United States, by PROSPERO, was a riveting true-life story of the lady who Did What Must Be Done with unparalleled New World style, charm—and enthusiasm!

With hindsight, the deliberate pace added so much. We knew each other rather well before our initial scene, and the whole phase of anticipation was a joy in itself. She had instructed me to purchase a large wooden hairbrush to present to her, and I had shared with her some of my other favourite novels, such as the classic Happy Tears, which she devoured in one night. She had written me in an early letter that her exploration of erotic fantasies combined three great interests of hers—psychology, sex, and literature. It also seemed clear that she enjoyed my inexperience as she told me at our last meeting before the first spanking that "you really will feel 12 again."

It was the closing of her next letter that virtually sent me over the edge:

Well, my boy, the moment is at hand. For years now you have deserved a sound spanking on your bare bottom and you know it. In just a few days you will be over my knee and I will be administering some old-fashioned discipline to you. I will, of course, spank you with my hand and with the hairbrush until your bottom is very red. Whether or not I use the strap depends on your willingness to submit completely to my authority—and to some extent on my mood. Certainly if you don't submit willingly, I will bend you over a chair and strap your bottom till you can't sit down for a week—I want that to be perfectly clear. In any event, you won't be sitting down comfortably for a day or two—but you will be assured that you are at last receiving the discipline you need. And you know that, although I am indeed very strict, I am also loving and fair.

I expect to see you at our usual meeting place at six o'clock on Thursday, August 31st. We will have a light supper and then… I shall leave the rest up to your imagination.

Pleasant dreams…

The scene itself lived up even to that billing. Vanessa was very theatrical and knew all the nuances of creating an intense fantasy. I was sent to the bedroom of her apartment to ponder my misdeeds while waiting for her arrival. When she entered the room, she first turned down the lighting. Dim lighting was a regular feature of our scenes, and many later spankings took place in candlelight. The lighting seemed to set just the right fantasy tone, as when we walked back into a well lit room after a scene we quickly reverted to our real life selves.

She then sat next to me on the bed and, using that firm but very feminine tone. explained to me how I was basically a good boy but needed discipline in my life, and it was now going to begin. I could only await her instructions. I was soon told to stand in front of her and not interfere as my belt was undone and trousers lowered. She then deftly bared my bottom just as she was easing me over her knee. Since I was to be rather "young" in this initial scene, the spanks were moderate at the most. I was simply to get a feel of what her discipline was to be like. She lectured me throughout, yet in soothing, almost loving, tones. Only when she picked up the hairbrush and first begin to apply its far greater sting did I respond out of turn by instantly reaching back with my hand to comfort a stinging bottom cheek. That serious breach of discipline was met with harder spanks. My frequent inability to keep from reaching back with my hands would lead to many similar reactions from her in the years to come.

I must have been over her knee for nearly a half hour that first session. When she finally let me rise, she told me to view my punished bottom in the mirror. Even in the dim light, her handiwork was apparent.

That night started well over four years of interludes across her knee. We continued to communicate primarily by letter—only using the phone for essential information. Variety was paramount. A business trip to London allowed me to acquire a genuine Lochgelly tawse, which she quickly put to good use. I also felt a handmade strap, a stinging metal ruler, and even a second hairbrush—sometimes all in one session. As I "grew older" in the relationship, the sessions became longer and much more severe. The lectures expanded and became more probing; the expected standards of behaviour were raised much higher. No aspect of adolescence was overlooked—ah, it was delightful.

And yet, there was so much more to make it all work. We'd always begin an evening together at an elegant restaurant in Boston or Cambridge (Massachusetts). Our conversation would be very much as adults with the emphasis on travel through our respective careers. She was very well known and well respected in her field of work. It was quite a thrill to wake up in a hotel one morning and watch my fantasy governess on national TV. Christmas would always bring an exchange of gifts, related to the obvious theme. I still remember her face when she opened her personalised stationery complete with her full fantasy name and PO Box on it.

Times change and so do lifestyles. In late 1982, I was offered a superb career opportunity which meant relocation. At the same time, I was going to become engaged that Christmas. When I told her my news at my apartment, she surprised me much more than I her by telling me that she too had just become engaged, as the right man for her had now entered her life. I was delighted by her good news, and our final scene that night was one of the longest and best ever. Perhaps our final night helped define what Vanessa really meant to me. Love can be felt in many ways, and one of the best is unselfishly. We clearly both felt happy for each other regarding the changes to come.

The word that seems to best sum up my feelings for her is that I adored her—and still do. In a very real sense, I looked up to her and felt very comfortable doing so. In turn, I felt her deep caring and warmth for me on a consistent basis.

She once wrote about the lifelong bond that existed between us; time has proven that true. We remain in regular touch, seeing each other for lunch once or twice a year. She has enriched my life and continues to do so. Today, almost 13 years after we first met, I still have trouble believing my good fortune.

The Art of the Cane & the Care of the Soul

***Miss Marianne* explains her philosophy and practice of the classic instrument of schoolroom discipline, in whose use she is an acknowledged adept.**

LET ME BEGIN by saying that I consider the cane to be a ritual instrument of punishment and purification, and, that if it is to be used at all, it must be used with maximum force.

There are plenty of other implements which either hurt less—the ruler, the slipper (as it can be used lightly), the switch, or, in a lightweight form, the strap. A switch, for those of you mystified by the term, is a long, straight piece of rattan (the flexible material of which canes are made) but without the traditional crook handle which makes a cane a cane and no other implement.

You may say to me that there are differing thicknesses and lengths of cane also. May not one of these be used lightly? Not by me. I consider it a sacrilege to use a cane in a feeble manner, and even the so-called Nursery cane—a short, thin cane meant for young children—carries a very surprising sting when wielded in my capable hands.

That is as it should be. A caning is meant to be feared by the recipient, and should be feared. There are a number of my pupils who, having received a few moderate strokes of the switch remain convinced they have received the cane. If they had received a caning there would be no likelihood of confusion, I assure you!

The most important aspect to using the cane, as I have already said, is that it must be used with full force, and this is achieved by lifting the arm well back (in a straight line from the pupil's bottom), bringing the cane down swiftly and forcibly, and, most importantly, imagining the follow through.

It is important to be intuitive and feeling about a caning, and not mechanical, but one should have in mind a following through of the stroke as in tennis, golf, karate and numerous other sports.

To "follow-through" a stroke means to imagine that it is finishing at about the pupil's shoulders and not stopping dead as it meets the surface (to do so is, in effect, a pulling back). This mental action is mirrored by the pupil's reaction. I train my pupils to open their minds to the fact that the stroke is not stopping dead at the bottom, and to feel its purifying flame throughout the body. This is experienced as a hot pain which sears through one's whole torso as far as the shoulders.

If one can open oneself mentally to feel this, the caning is much more effective as a purifying force, and a great deal of inner guilt, cloudiness of mind and tension can be cleared away in one stroke.

Of course, needless to say, I do not usually give one stroke. A caning should be six of the best, or occasionally, if deserved, more. However, I generally prefer to keep to the traditional six strokes and to vary the heaviness of the cane if a more severe punishment is called for.

The whole atmosphere of a caning should be ritualistic. The announcement of the punishment, the command to rise and bend over the desk—with girls, the ceremonial lifting of the skirt and tucking in of the petticoat to make a smooth, tight surface—all these little things combine to make an awe inspiring atmosphere before the cane is raised. I also tap the cane lightly on the recipient's bottom a few times before each stroke. This gives me a guide for the aim of my eye, a practice stroke in miniature, and increases apprehension in the pupil.

Incidentally, before I close, let me say that although I do often use the cane on girls, many of those in my charge (or who visit me) escape my final penalty because I consider them rather too sensitive for one of my canings; but all the same many girls can and do accept quite hard punishments, and nearly always with less fuss than a boy. This is a generalisation of course, but as I expect my punishments to be received in a respectful silence appropriate to the ritual nature of the occasion, I am often better pleased by the response of the so called weaker sex than of the stronger. With this thought, I leave you to speculate whether you would accept a caning from me in a dignified and proper manner—or otherwise!

FROM THE ARCHIVES

From *HOOD'S OWN* or
LAUGHTER FROM YEAR TO YEAR
Edward Moxon, London 1855.

Here, come, Master Timothy Todd,
Before we have done you'll look grimmer
You've been spelling some time for the rod,
And your jacket shall know I'm a Trimmer.

You don't know your A from your B,
So backward you are in your Primer:
Don't kneel—you shall go on my knee,
For I'll have you to know I'm a Trimmer.

This morning you hinder'd the cook,
By melting your dumps in the skimmer;
Instead of attending your book—
But I'll have you to know I'm a Trimmer.

To-day, too, you went to the pond,
And bathed, though you are not a swimmer;
And with parents so doting and fond—
But I'll have you to know I'm a Trimmer.

After dinner you went to the wine,
And help'd yourself—yes, to a brimmer;
You couldn't walk straight in a line,
But I'll make you to know I'm a Trimmer.

You kick little Tomkins about,
Because he is slighter and slimmer;
Are the weak to be thump'd by the stout?
But I'll have you to know I'm a Trimmer.

ilfering

's call you
r—
ne if
!
ou to know
rimmer.

ade game at

that my
rown
r,
t I watch'd you,
e got a sly
nack !
And I'll have
o know I'm a
mmer

Don't think that my temper is hot,
It's never beyond a slow simmer;
I'll teach you to call me Dame Trot,
But I'll have you to know I'm a Trimmer.

Miss Edgeworth, or Mrs. Chapone,
Might melt to behold your tears glimmer;
Mrs. Barbauld would let you alone,
But I'll have you to know I'm a Trimmer.

From the Archives

My school days began when I was four and a half years old. There were no public schools in Missouri in those early days but there were two private schools—terms twenty-five cents per week per pupil and collect it if you can. Mrs. Horr taught the children in a small log house at the southern end of Main Street. Mr. Sam Cross taught the young people of larger growth in a frame school-house on the hill. I was sent to Mrs. Horr's school and I remember my first day in that little log house with perfect clearness, after these sixty-five years and upwards—at least I remember an episode of that first day. I broke one of the rules and was warned not to do it again and was told that the penalty for a second breach was a whipping. I presently broke the rule again and Mrs. Horr told me to go out and find a switch and fetch it. I was glad she appointed me, for I believed I could select a switch suitable to the occasion with more judiciousness than anybody else.

In the mud I found a cooper's shaving of the old time pattern, oak, two inches broad, a quarter of an inch thick, and rising in a shallow curve at one end. There were nice new shavings of the same breed close by but I took this one, although it was rotten. I carried it to Mrs. Horr, presented it and stood before her in an attitude of meekness and resignation which seemed to me calculated to win favour and sympathy, but it did not happen. She divided a long look of strong disapprobation equally between me and the shaving; then she called me by my entire name, Samuel Langhorne Clemens—probably the first time I had ever heard it all strung together in one procession—and said she was ashamed of me. I was to learn later that when a teacher calls a boy by his entire name it means trouble. She said she would try and appoint a boy with a better judgment than mine in the matter of switches, and it saddens me yet to remember how many faces lighted up with the hope of getting that appointment. Jim Dunlap got it and when he returned with the switch of his choice I recognised that he was an expert.

From The Autobiography of Mark Twain

ISSUE 3

DIVINATION AS A METHOD OF ASSESSING PUNISHMENT

Clairvoyante faculties, trust in a Higher Power and a pack of playing cards are all one needs to make those difficult disciplinary judgements, says XANTHIA

I HAVE NOTICED of late how little attention is paid, by commentators and admirers, to the mystical overtones of Miss Kerr-Sutherland's wonderful *Guide*. It is almost as if there is a conspiracy to ignore them.

Her whole Tripartite System (of Nurse, Matron and Crone) is so obviously derived from classical paganism that it is hard to imagine her other insights could have been evolved without a degree of clairvoyance, for she perceives (accurately) that all women who administer discipline do so, ultimately, not in their own right, but as Servants of a Higher Power. They are, as she rightly says, Priestesses and Mediums.

There are many occasions when the disciplining female will be unsure of what to do concerning a particular punishment. We all have these times of diminished insight. Rather than administer an unjust or badly calculated award, a better system is to remember that we, too, have a Power to call upon in times of doubt—and then to call upon it.

I am a clairvoyante and for some years now I have used an ordinary pack of playing cards to determine the quality and style of a punishment, when I myself am unsure, and I should like to explain my system so that other ladies with similar gifts may do the same.

The first thing is to remove all Jokers and

Kings from the pack. They play no part in the divination.

Shuffle the pack and order the culprit to cut seven times.

Deal the cards one after the other until the first Queen appears. This card represents the Mistress (you). Set it aside. It forms the first tableau.

Now hand the pack to the culprit and instruct him to deal cards singly until a Knave appears. This card represents the Delinquent (him). Set it directly underneath the Queen on the table. It forms the second tableau.

Now remove all remaining Knaves and Queens from the pack and shuffle again, three times. The culprit should cut the pack.

Calculate the month numerically (e.g. 1 to 12). Deal off that number of cards. The last you dealt is placed on the right of the Knave and forms the third tableau.

Calculate the day of the month numerically (1 to 31). Deal off that many cards. Place the last-dealt card to the right of the others. This forms the fourth tableau.

Calculate the hour of the day (1 to 12, not 1 to 24!). Deal an appropriate number of cards. Continue the row to the right. This forms the fifth tableau.

Calculate the minute of the hour. You will probably have to gather in the discards (without shuffling) and keep dealing if this number is very high. Repeat if necessary. This forms the sixth tableau.

Calculate the second of the minute—it is best to use a watch with a second hand. Extend the row to the seventh and final tableau.

It goes without saying that this ritual should be conducted in perfect, reverent silence: After all, you are asking for help.

The first tableau stands for you, the Mistress, and is immutable.

The second tableau stands for the culprit.

The third tableau stands for the general

tone of the punishment, calculated on a scale of 1 to 10 (aces are always low), with 1 representing the harshest aspect of your personality and 10 the most compassionate. Use it as a guide for your own personal demeanour throughout the chastisement.

The fourth tableau stands for the physical severity of the punishment, again on a scale of 1 to 10, with 1 being the most severe and 10 the most lenient.

The fifth tableau stands for the degree of humiliation which must be applied, on the same scale (1 = acute, 10 = very mild). I generally interpret this to refer to the mode of preparation for punishment. A 10 in this tableau would suggest to me that the culprit be allowed to retain all his clothes for the punishment, and be allowed to assume the necessary posture of his own volition; also for privacy to reign. A 1 I might interpret as the most humiliating circumstances I could devise—certainly a bare bottom, possibly

petticoated beforehand, and in public if at all convenient.

The sixth tableau refers to the implement to be used. Here only the suit is important, with ♠ = a birch-rod, ♦ = a cane, ♣ = a strap or paddle, and ♥ = the palm of the hand. (It is obviously important to have samples of these weapons to hand.)

The seventh tableau refers to the number of strokes to be administered, subject to the following modifications:

If tableau six = ♠ then there are no modifications to the total. If it = ♦ then multiply tableau seven by two; if it = ♣ then multiply tableau seven by three. If it = ♥ then multiply tableau seven by four. Thus the maximum punishment that can be administered with a birch is 10 strokes, the maximum with a cane 20 strokes, the maximum with strap or tawse is 30 strokes, and the maximum spanking with the palm—40 smacks.

There are other minor variations which may be read from the cards. If Tableaus one and two are the same colour, the punishment should be inflicted immediately. If they are not the same colour, it should be deferred to an appointed time.

Using the above system, let us divine the punishment decreed by the following cards:

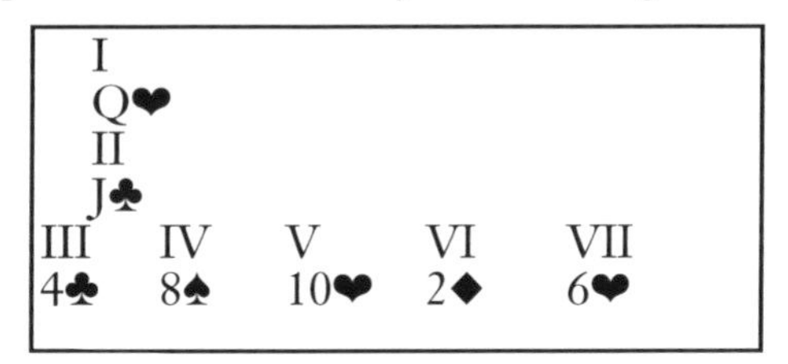

	I			
	Q♥			
	II			
	J♣			
III	IV	V	VI	VII
4♣	8♠	10♥	2♦	6♥

III. The tone of the punishment is rather severe—a cold, precise and forbidding demeanour would be appropriate.

IV. Physical severity is on the low side; you need not strike particularly hard (though firmly).

V. Humiliation is not a factor in the punishment—the culprit must be allowed to retain as much dignity as possible.

VI. Use of the cane is indicated.

VII. 12 strokes (6 x 2).

So the final picture emerges; a punishment which, after an interval of waiting, is set in hand as if it is going to be a harsh one, but is in practice a moderate dozen on the seat of the trousers or the back of the skirt—in private.

Obviously some culprits will come in time to guess these rules for Reading; in which case I suggest you occasionally reverse the normal order of harsh–mild—normally this runs from 1 to 10 but can if you wish be set to run 10 to 1. Do not tell the culprit in advance which system you propose to use! (Work out for yourselves how the above punishment would alter.)

Trust the Readings and act upon them faithfully. Devise your own and note the results.

May Our Threefold Lady shine the Light of Her Knowledge upon you.

THE ONCE AND FUTURE CANE

Stings Aren't What They Used To Be, Concludes Miss Alicia *of The Wildfire Club.*

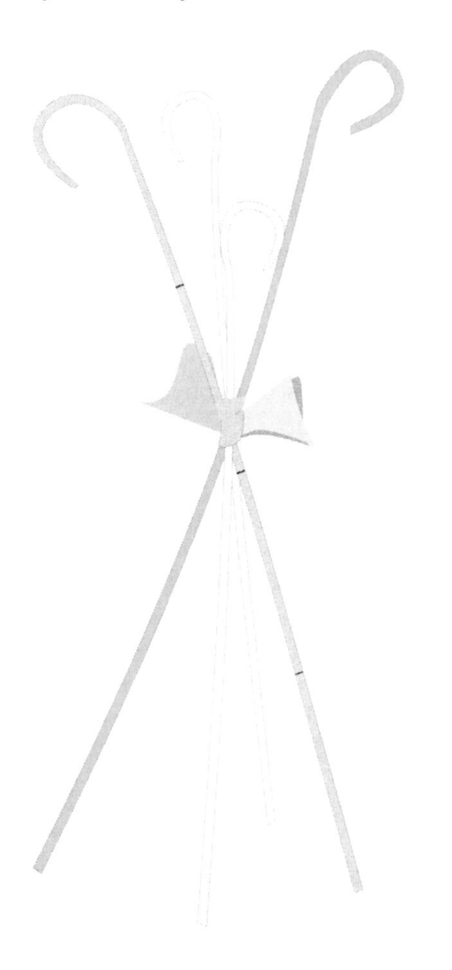

A good, sound caning depends upon a good, sound cane. The trouble is that in the latter part of the 20th century good canes are increasingly difficult to come by. There are, of course, various suppliers offering what they describe as "school canes": but any one who has used the real school canes sold by scholastic suppliers, or who has been caned at school or by a traditional governess, will easily recognise that the modern implements have little of the quality of the real school cane.

The difference may seem hard to place—the length, weight and thickness are similar; the handle may be well shaped (though often it is not)—yet that indefinable combination of density and suppleness, that almost fluid quality which gives the penetrating sting, the patina and balance of the true English school cane—all seem to be missing.

The late 20th century cane, like the late 20th century itself, seems somehow substandard; and the various ladies of my acquaintance have tended to think of canes as they think of nylons; just as the only really good nylons are those one manages to find still in unopened packets from the 1950s and early 1960s (there are more of them about than you might imagine), so the only really good canes are the surviving ones that can be acquired from old school stocks.

Yet surely there must be an answer to both problems. Surely a manufacturer of stockings could, if he wished, produce that beautiful, filmy quality of nylon which is absent from even the most expensive of late 20th century stockings; and surely canes made in the late 20th century could have the sheen and strength and fluid suppleness of a real school cane?

Well, the stocking problem will have to remain unsolved for a few years longer, none of us being experts in synthetics (though if any of our readers is an expert in synthetics and can offer advice on the manufacture of real stockings he may be able to confer an ineffable benefit upon the human species).

The cane problem, on the other hand, has been resolved in the most satisfactory manner possible.

What is it that differentiates a good cane from a mediocre one? Although the problem puzzled us for some time, the answer is really quite obvious when you think about it. It is the quality of the cane itself. Canes, of course are made from an Oriental stem called rattan, but is a little known fact that there are many hundreds of varieties of rattan, all with curious Oriental names, such as Boonloot and "Dragon", only a few of which are really suitable for the manufacture of disciplinary instruments. The traditional makers of scholastic canes had their cane specially selected, while the modern cane maker for the "adult" market simply purchases his cane from handicraft suppliers, thus getting a grade which is ideally suited to—well, handicrafts, but hardly ideal for the purpose to which it is being put.

We are pleased to report that we have now located sources of traditional school quality cane, and are able to make both Junior and Senior School Canes (Junior canes are not only thinner than senior ones but are actually made from a different variety of rattan) to order.

The Junior Cane is a light, whippy implement, deceptively slight in appearance, but with a breathtaking sting.

The Office Cane, which is essentially a longer and slightly heavier version of the Junior School Cane is intended for young ladies of working age and may be used over the skirt with the most keenly penetrating effect (see *The Female Disciplinary Manual* for further information on classes of cane).

The Senior School Cane is a more robust implement altogether, although it is still extremely flexible. This is really a standard cane—"getting the cane" would normally refer to receiving a set number of strokes from a cane of this type, and "six of the best" from a Senior School cane is a punishment which will not easily be forgotten.

Readers of *The Female Disciplinary Manual* will be familiar with the concept of a "Victorian" cane. This is a cane made from a very particular grade of rattan: mid-to-dark brown (rather than yellowish) in colour and combining the texture and finish of a hard wood with a quite remarkable degree of suppleness. Canes of this sort were more familiar in Victorian times than they are now, and were perhaps chief among the things which made a Victorian governess feared, respected and instantly obeyed. Collectors of traditional school canes will have come across such implements which stand out from the general run.

We have discovered that these Victorian canes are, in fact, made from a special grade of rattan which is no longer commercially grown (although it was in Victorian times). The natives gather lengths of it which they find growing wild in the forests and every now and again they make up their gleanings into a bale which is sold to the West.

Such a bale was received this year, but we have been told that the last time such a bale was available was some fifteen years ago, and there is no telling when one may be available again. As soon as we discovered this, we bought up the remainder of the bale.

Our main Victorian cane is aptly named "The Governess", a fearsome, though quite slender, implement suitable for use by a lady with uncompromising standards. Owing to the fact that the cane is expensive and very rare, "The Governess" is not cheap; nor do we recommend her for use on people unaccustomed to traditional discipline; but for those who desire a true, disciplinary cane of, so to speak, the old school, this cane is very highly recommended.

"The Governess" should not be used for regular canings—for these, the implements described earlier are more than adequate, but where the ultimate sanction of a really sound chastisement is required, it is an excellent idea to have a cane of this nature—kept perhaps in a cupboard or on top of a wardrobe—to be brought out when required.

We have other Victorian canes. The heavy Penal Cane should in our view never be used on females—and we are not sure about any one else! It is a very severe implement, long, thick and flexible. We make it available simply because we know that it cannot be obtained elsewhere, but sell it with the warning that it is not for most people.

Finally, my favourite cane of all, the one we call "The Lady Cane": this is a Victorian cane, like "the Governess", but of an extraordinary slenderness and flexibility; dark and hard as a walking stick, and of about the same length, yet no thicker than a pencil, this cane is perfect for the most elegant lady, who with its aid would administer, almost effortlessly, punishment of the sharpest and most effective kind. Regrettably, Victorian cane of this kind is so rare that our small supplies of it have already been taken up by ladies within our own circle; however if we ever again able to acquire cane of this kind we shall make it available to others.

A Caning Ceremony resembles an Act of Religious Devotion, in the opinion of MARCUS.

MISS MARIANNE'S ARTICLE in the second issue of *The Governess* is valuable for drawing our attention to the fact that caning is very much an art form; not just because of the importance attached to the need to be accurate when administering a caning, but because the very act of corporal punishment is a ritual. It requires considerable sensitivity on the part of the punisher to ensure that the punishment is acted out with the full sense of necessary ritual. Anyone can administer a caning, but it takes no little skill to administer a punishment with the proper sense of drama. Readers who have seen the canings administered in the films *If* and *Another Country* will be aware of the ceremony that often attended public school canings.

Why is it necessary that corporal punishment be so ritualised? The short answer is that ritual increases both fear and shame on the part of the offending pupil. He is therefore less likely to forget the punishment, and the reason why he is being punished. A public caning is almost inevitably likely to be ritualistic. Before (and possibly even after) the Second World War, it was not uncommon for boys in public schools to be caned or birched in public, in front of the entire school at assembly. I even once read of a case where public canings took place in a girls' school. There is a particularly interesting passage from Frank Richards' *Billy Bunter's Banknote*

THE IMPORTANCE OF RITUAL IN PHYSICAL PUNISHMENT

describing the public birching of Herbert Vernon-Smith, the 'cad' of the Remove and one of Bunter's fellow pupils.

> The last resounding swish of the birch had died away through the silent Hall. From Herbert Vernon-Smith, not a sound had come.
>
> Hall was packed. Every fellow of every form was there, from Sixth Form seniors down to fags of the Second Form—the Prefects in their places, with their canes under their arms: the masters, with grave faces: the hapless culprit, quiet and subdued, but with a hint of defiance in his glinting eyes. A public flogging was a rare occasion at Greyfriars in latter days—the hard old days were long gone when that ancient hall had often echoed to the swishing of the birch in the hands of grim old headmasters and the painful howls of the victims. Greyfriars men were 'whopped' when they required the same, but 'six on the bags' in a study was the usual limit. Only on very rare occasions—very rare indeed—was there a public 'execution': with the school assembled in the Hall, masters and boys all present, and the culprit 'hoisted' in the old-fashioned way—and no doubt it was all the more impressive for that reason.

Miss Marianne writes of caning having a cleansing and purifying effect on a pupil. This notion is connected to the idea that a ritualised caning is strongly suggestive of a religious act of atonement. A caning is thus an act of sacrifice. One may regard the piece of furniture over which the pupil bends as an altar. The governess who administers the punishment plays the part of a priestess. The role of the priestess will be enhanced if the governess wears the traditional black teacher's gown and academic cap. Indeed, such garb should always be worn by governesses when they administer punishment, in order to create the necessary sense of ceremony. If punishment on the bare bottom has been ordained, then the removal of clothing naturally constitutes a part of this ceremony, and may be seen as preparing the 'victim' for sacrifice. Finally, the sacrifice is consummated by the caning.

As many school canings that took place in public often followed school assembly, the religious connection was strengthened by the punishment taking place directly after an act of religious worship. It will be noted that Alice Kerr-Sutherland regarded her punishment room as a chapel, so further reinforcing the idea of corporal punishment as an atoning act of sacrifice.

Miss Marianne's comments on silence during a caning are of great interest. Such a silence is, as she described it, 'respectful'. To take a thrashing in silence indicates that the pupil accepts his punishment is deserved. It also indicates that he understands and accepts the importance and the beauty of a ceremonial thrashing, even though the punishment itself is feared and not desired. An exception to this rule may be when the pupil is required to count aloud the strokes as he receives them—in a normal voice, which should not betray any indication of pain. At the end of the punishment this might be followed by an expression of gratitude. Some governesses may also find it desirable for the pupil to fetch and hand over the cane before bending over. In addition the pupil's obedient response to the command 'bend over' (and to remove clothing if this is desired) forms an essential part of compliance to the ritual. Those who have been caned in this way will be aware that it takes considerable willpower not to cry out or to stand up. The demonstration of such willpower by a pupil is a clear example that he is sensitive to the spiritual aspects of corporal punishment. It need hardly be said that a pupil who does cry out, stand up or struggle during a punishment should receive extra strokes of the utmost severity until he learns to display the correct attitude.

One who complains or sulks about his chastisement afterwards may be considered a fitting candidate for further punishment and should be so warned. Tears may of course be shed, but only after the punishment, and in private. ✣

FROM THE ARCHIVES

"He is a young savage, this master Hugh Dysart, and from the first he has continually done all he dared to defy and annoy me. But yesterday the crisis arrived. He brought into the school-room a dog I hate (and secretly stand in fear of), a big fierce-looking creature... and he also brought a whip with which he teased it. I ordered the dog out, and told him to bring the whip to me. He told the dog to remain, and refused to bring me the whip. I am afraid of the dog, as I tell you, but my temper was stronger than my fear; so I went to the animal and took it boldly by its collar and led it out myself. Then I returned to my seat and commanded my young Sir Roderick to come to me, as I had done before. The two girls dropped their books, and sat and stared at me. I really believe there was something in my face which frightened them. For fully two minutes the boy sat in his seat, laughing at me... and then a sudden passion of fury seemed to seize upon him. He sprang up and ran towards me, all at once, and before I could touch him his whip had struck me across my face.

"You cannot imagine, unless you have once received such a blow, what its effect was upon me. My temper is not a cold one, and between the sting and the humiliation, and my perfect conviction that my time had come, I will confess that it got the better of me. In two seconds I had wrenched the whip from the little animal's hand, and held him with all my strength, and then I beat him—and beat him—and beat him! I beat him until I felt that even the amiable Sir Roderick might have considered I had distinguished myself; after which exploit I flung him upon the floor, broke the whip into half a dozen pieces, and threw it at him where he lay..."

Frances Hodgson Burnett:
A Woman's Will (1863)

Feminæ Amez Verite

Do Englishwomen have the stomach to Do What Must Be Done? MARIE-ANTOINETTE *is highly doubtful…*

ONE READS THROUGH *The Governess* with great delight. Many of the articles ring so very true when one believes, as I do, that the male sex deserves and requires the strictest discipline. It is sad, however, to see that the majority of Englishwomen are still so submissive—almost slaves to their menfolk.

The motto of our family, once cousins to William the Conqueror, was always Amez Verite, or "Love the Truth", and I do wish women would take such a motto seriously instead of the pretences and false claims they so often make.

I firmly believe that as far as capabilities go, and certainly in regard to strength of will, health and longevity, Woman is superior to Man but has been held back for some 3,000 years in a false Patriarchal society until she has lost faith and belief in herself. To this very end, several years ago I and my sisters founded in France "The Order of Isabelle", which we named after our famous and beloved ancestress Queen Isabelle, Princess of France and wife of King Edward II of England, who was firm and dominant in every way. We had as our objective the total superiority of the female and a belief in strict rules and Discipline for Society. Since Society is, and has been for some thousands of years, male dominated, this means the majority in need of strict rules and discipline are males.

Success was easy in France, Germany and the USA, where girls are not "doormats" and will not tolerate wife-beaters, drunkards and gamblers; but in England women are so very docile. It is pathetic to hear a woman in Court saying, tearfully, when her bigamous husband is sent down, "I will wait for him until he comes out", or to see a woman suffering beatings and abuse for years and still declaring love. The way so many females allow themselves to be sexually abused, taunted and subjected to obscene suggestions in this day and age is, to put it mildly, pathetic.

If one turns to the media one can see hundreds of advertisements said to be inserted by women. They claim to be Mistresses, very dominant, very strict, ready to teach male slaves to behave and obey. They say they can and will use whip, cane and paddle to enforce their will until one feels the birches of Governesses are almost childish toys.

How wonderful it it were true, that there

were genuine, non-fee-seeking, dominant girls and women who loved teaching men to behave, to obey strict rules, and could enforce discipline by birch, cane or tawse—but it is all false.

Should a male make contact with such claimants they will find a façade hiding a fee-seeking and play-acting prostitute. My own researches in England have shown that so far I have not truly found a woman who is really dominant, who believes in discipline, is able to apply the birch and cane to the proper place. Always they have some weak excuse, until I would go so far as to declare: "in England no genuine strict Governess type of female exists". This makes me very sad.

What has this female "wishy-washy" attitude created? A Society where men feel that every woman is a chattel, is there for the purpose of accepting sex, whether by being pawed around in marriage or raped by a man wanting sex. To have no freedom to dress as she pleases at work, for short skirts on shapely legs are a "come on" and a show of knickers drives them wild. She is forced by her own weakness to dress to please him not herself, to watch what he wants on TV, and to cook and slave for someone far less intelligent, far less worthy and far less loveable than herself.

What if the shoe were on the other foot? What if we demanded sex from them every hour or so? What if we raped them for a change? What if we found their dress sexually exciting and taunted them? The world would be a better place.

Today mothers cannot chastise their sons, women teachers cannot upbraid the misbehaving youth with birch or cane—and what have the Do-Gooders achieved? Lawless behaviour in schools, young female teachers raped by boys of thirteen, teachers afraid to teach, surrendering a worthwhile profession.

The lack of discipline even enters the Police Force where young policewomen are treated as sex objects (some have even suffered rape).

Truly present day attitudes, two thousand years after Christ, are unbelievable. The Church of England and the Roman Church debates and refuses—or accepts under protest—women priests; whereas for thousands of years Priestesses alone administered to the Mother Goddess. Even after Christ Himself had kept company with women and stood up for their rights, even when the early Gospels are full of Female Disciples and followers holding office, they still cling to their false male superiority. Would they have had a Master without Mary? Who refused to flee at the Crucifixion? And who first declared the story of the Resurrection? Women.

So again I ask women to believe in the ideals of *The Governess*, to remember the motto Feminæ amez verite, and do not pretend to be dominant unless you mean it. Do not declare yourselves believers in the Birch unless you are ready to apply it to the seats of unruly sons and disobedient husbands. Shake off the Fetters of parochial times, be what you are, Superior in all respects to the Male; and force your way into the highest administrative posts.

Do not allow yourselves to be sexual playthings, dictated to on abortion by men, told what you can read or watch by the male sex; and do not allow yourselves to be beaten by these creatures or raped because you wish to take a walk in the twilight and dressed in the way you wish even if it displays your loveliness. In the home apply the principles of *The Governess* to sons at an early age, for the birch will create a far better citizen later on.

I am looking forward to the day when Englishwomen are truly dominant, good with birch and tawse, in reality and not in cheap advertisements or on cards left in phone booths, and when they are not using their beauty as fodder for Girlie magazines and "Page Three". ✤

THE FRENCH Have A Word For It

By JACQUELINE OPHIR

SEVERAL OF YOU who have written to me in connexion with the serial *The House in St. John's Wood* have voiced surprise that I make such free use of French phraseology. Is English not the language of discipline? demands one Member. And, that being so, why do I not avail myself of it? The word *pretentious*, while not actually uttered (sensible chap!), is clearly trembling on his lips.

The answer is that while *Anglo-Saxonisme* (!), taken as a whole, may well be the dominant culture where physical discipline is concerned, English is not the best designed language. It may surprise many to know that French is somewhat superior—that is, there are more words (and more of these are specific) than in English to describe the processes and techniques of discipline.

In view of the traditional view held by the French (nation), that physical discipline is *un vice anglaise* (a French phrase and notion which has gone around the world), this might seem odd. In my opinion this ancient libel is an excellent piece of camouflage designed to obfuscate the fact that the same *vice* (*à propos*, I do not for one moment accept that it is a vice) is well and truly *française*.

Similar examples of "Displaced Guilt" are common in history. The voluble 19th-century American denigration of British "imperialism" conveniently pushed aside the fact that in the same period the USA was busily building up its own huge land (and later maritime) empire, using methods no less ruthless than the British (ask any Red Indian or Mexican). The Soviet Russians similarly denounced American "imperialism", despite having inherited (and retained) the largest land empire in the world, a legacy of the Tsars. And while the French were busily concocting the myth of the *vice anglaise*, they were themselves practising physical discipline as assiduously (and artistically) as any. It may even be true to say that the most refined of all "national" approaches to this subject is that defined by our gifted neighbours across the Channel.

If I were truly bilingual, French is the language I would choose in which to write a story about Discipline. There are simply more words to use. One of the best known is *fessée* (v. *fesser*, n. *fesses* "buttocks"). Its meaning is equivalent to "a spanking" (literally "bottom-ing"), but it can also be used for any form of corporal discipline applied to the hinder parts (whereas "spanking" has several meanings, not all of which refer to discipline at all; e.g. "a spanking new car"). *Clacquer* (an obvious sample of Gallic onomatopœia) also means "to spank", though the use of the palm is strongly implied with this particular verb, as in the English "smack".

The generic word for all forms of rear-end punishment is the racily onomatopœic *fouetter*, to whip; but here "whip" is used in the same antique sense that it once held in England and America, and does not necessarily mean that a whip is used. The French term for the apocryphal beldame who rules by the rod (and it is interesting in itself that this term exists) is *Mére Fouettard*, while their delightful colloquialism for a punishment inflicted across the knee is *à maman* ("mama-style").

Then there is the beautiful French name for the instrument that, in historical times, was the most likely to be chosen for any *bonne fessée: La Verge*, the rod (Lat. *virga*), usually taken to mean a birch-rod, though properly this should be *une verge de boileau*. Once again, this is an exact equivalent to the old meaning for rod in English; simply a weapon of chastisement, and while most probably a birch-rod, not necessarily so.

The cane being less favoured in French schools and homes, there are fewer words for this implement: *la canne* is the proper term, but the colloquialism (again, interesting that one should exist at all) is *la baguette*, the stick, used today exclusively to describe the characteristic long French loaf.

The French, of course, have their own "national" instrument of correction, *le martinet* or short-tailed domestic cat o' nine (or six) tails.

However, as one might expect from the French, it is in the specific language of preparation for punishment—in other words, the undressing, partial or otherwise, of a culprit—that our neighbours' tongue excels in precision.

Consider the useful verb *déculotter*—a single word meaning "to take down the trousers (or pants)", whose noun equivalent, *la déculottage*, is nearly as useful. (There is also *réculotter*, meaning to replace or button up the garment in question.) In an earlier period of English, there was once a precise equivalent: unbreech. But this has now fallen from use ("debag" carries an entirely different meaning, with connotations of male horseplay), and in order to give this fatal command the Anglo-Saxon disciplinarienne is obliged to employ an entire phrase, where her Gallic cousin simply says "*Déculottes-toi!*". Nor is this the only term available to her: if she wishes, she may say "*Baissez!*" (meaning "Down with 'em!"), or "*Retroussez!*" meaning "tuck it up!"

Down with what? If we are discussing the principal garment, we say "trousers" or, if we are American, "pants". (If an Englishwoman says "take down your pants" she is referring to the underwear. If she tells a culprit to undo his "suspenders", she is referring to a strange and almost forgotten elastic device used by gentlemen of an earlier and more stylish era to hold up their socks—whereas if she is American she means what an Englishwoman would call the braces [Fr. *bretelles*].)

Here French is actually more confusing than Anglo-American, since *culottes* (cf. *déculotter*) can mean shorts, trousers or knickers, but then, so can *pantalon*.

But French inventiveness does not cease there, as the wide range of materials used for the manufacture of *une verge* testifies: birch *(boileau)* is the favourite, in France as everywhere, but heather *(brùyere)*, broom *(genêt)*, and even holly *(houx)* may be chosen, though the last-named is questionable for practical use.

Perhaps the most famous French *verge de specialité* is a rod made from nettles *(orties)*; it sounds fearsome, but is said to have greater aphrodisiac than punitive properties—and that, as readers will readily agree, sounds French enough to be true. ✤

RETURN OF THE CLASSROOM HORSE

AN EXPERIMENT BY PRIMULA

LIKE ALL WHO have read the admirable *Guide To The Correction Of Young Gentlemen*, I have nothing but praise for it. I thought, however, that I would pick out a very small topic, which has particular significance for me, that is to say, Horsing. I have only found a very limited amount of information on this subject in the book.

Recently I was in the fortunate position of reviewing my previously negative thoughts on this mode of chastisement by putting them to a practical test.

My main objection to horsing had

How it was done in Ancient Rome. From a Pompeiian wall frieze.

stemmed from my own practical experience—always the best guide, I think. I once found myself in the shameful position of being ordered to accept a punishment in this manner. My corrector ordered a young gentleman of slight build to take me on his back. This was a new experience for both of us and naturally both of us were nervous in our different ways. The young man stooped a little and took hold of both of my wrists, pulling forward as he did so. This resulted in my feet being lifted off the ground by only a few feet. With impatient urging from the disciplinarian the "horse" struggled to lean forward, making sounds of obvious distress. My skirts were quickly raised by the master and with some considerable haste he administered the promised twelve strokes of the tawse—not at all accurately, I fear, due mainly to the instability of my "horse".

For my part I found the whole affair most unsatisfactory. I have to admit that the fear of falling and injuring myself, or the young man (or even both), by far outweighed the pain of the actual beating—just as the worry of looking ridiculous sprawled in a heap on the floor outweighed any graver humiliation. Respect for the disciplinarian also suffered.

So is it small wonder that, as a Mistress in a position of corporal authority over young men and women, I had never yet chosen this method? Even reading others' (more successful) experiences of the horsing procedure, and in full knowledge of long tradition, I still found it hard to visualise it as the best position to administer my most favoured of punishment rods; that is to say, the magnificent Birch! It seemed to me that the target would be at an undesirable—i.e. too "flat"—angle.

But I have never been one publicly to decry (or approve) a procedure until I have had first hand experience. I therefore decided that at the earliest opportunity I would find out if my prejudices held true in practice.

What Miss Kerr-Sutherland had to say:

"To mount a culprit on a horse, [the assistant] takes him on her back with his arms pulled forward and down across her shoulders and his wrists tightly gripped; his face is thus pressed up against the back of her neck. She then stoops well forward; his weight is brought directly over hers, making the burden easier to bear than it seems to an onlooker; and his bottom is brought into a presentation that, for angle, elevation and convenience, is unsurpassed. He is perfectly helpless, with his hands held and his legs impeded from kicking by his fallen clothes (which should be left around the knees for this very purpose)."

A Guide to the Correction of Young Gentlemen

Quite recently I acquired a very robust maid, well over six feet tall (rather like Dorothy Baxter in *The House in St. John's Wood*) and solidly built (to say the least). With six young men and two young ladies in my charge for a short term's tuition I felt sure her assistance would provide me with the opportunity I desired.

As I had suspected, by the end of term I had three young men and one young lady who had amassed more than the allowed total of classroom punishments and demerits. I felt totally justified, therefore, one morning, in announcing to the class that there would be a formal traditional punishment for the four pupils before prep that day.

At the end of lessons the class were told to remain in their seats. I then rang for the maid, who had of course been instructed in her new duties the previous night.

The first culprit called out—a young

How it was done in 19th century British Public Schools

man—was of light build. On being instructed to do so, he faced the class and recited aloud the list of crimes that had led him to this sorry pass. He was not, I think, over-surprised when I announced that he was to receive twelve strokes of the birch: however there was a look of alarm on his face (as well as those of his three fellow culprits) when I announced that they were all to be horsed and birched for their misdeeds!

The first delinquent was then ordered to unbutton his trousers and raise his arms—his shorts inevitably fell to his ankles. The maid advanced, turned her back to the class, ducked a little as she took hold of the culprit's wrists, and pulled forward at the same time. The culprit was lifted a foot or so off the floor. To my surprise I then found his bottom at just the right height for a good accurate stroke to be administered.

The "horse" stood rock solid throughout and I had no cause for haste. On completion of the birching she merely dipped a little in order to return the young man to the ground—where he promptly knelt to render gratitude for his whipping by kissing first the birch, then my hand. In deference to Etonian tradition, he was then presented with the birch, which he ruefully took back to his desk.

Recipient number two was a young man of more solid build, though of no great height. When told to take up the same position as the previous malcontent he found that he could not reach high enough for the maid to take hold of his hands; she had to bend her knees into a crouching position in order to get a firm grasp of the culprit's wrists. Standing upright, she then found herself unbalanced, so she instinctively leaned well forwards. The culprit was therefore hoisted far higher than the previous recipient, and in a much less vertical position, almost akin to being bent over a gym horse. He was, however, inclined to wave his legs erratically, until I raised his trousers to knee-level and buttoned them up. This served to constrain his legs, thereby avoiding a moving target, and any danger of destabilisation.

I was then able to administer a very forceful and accurate birching, with the rod the culprit himself had previously made. (It has always been my policy to have the birch "put up" by the recidivist for whom it is intended.) I was also given to understand, by the "horse", that the latter culprit, though heavier, and his punishment more prolonged (eighteen strokes), had in fact been the easier of the two (so far) to mount and support.

I had observed for myself that the second miscreant had found his beating more painful and that the marks left by the birch were more visible.

19th century classroom horsings (of both sexes) are shewn in these two illustrations of the period. Despite the differences in technique, the drawings are almost identical—could they be by the same artist, or was this a common spectacle with its own accepted visual conventions?

The last pair to be disciplined are of particular interest in this experiment as I felt that my researches would be extended in a charming manner if a young man were to be made to horse a young lady. This way it would also serve as an extra lesson for the young lady as she had been particularly rude and unkind to the young man also about to be disciplined. The pair were of approximately equal build.

They were called up together and approached with looks of apprehension and puzzlement on their faces. I informed them both what I had planned. On learning she was to be horsed on the back of her classmate for twelve strokes of the birch, the female miscreant visibly paled and her lower lip began to tremble. As for me, I was curious to see how the young man would manage someone of his own size. However he had obviously been paying close attention to the earlier punishments, and chose to follow the example of the second of these. He bent his knees and took up a crouching position before he took hold of the girl's wrists, making sure they were pulled well down on his chest before he arose. Once he had risen and leaned forward a little it was clear that he had the young lady very secure: she was held well up with her head almost brushing his ear. When I was satisfied that they were both steady and in no danger of toppling over, I instructed the maid, who was standing by, to prepare the culprit in the usual manner for females.

I felt it appropriate that the young lady should receive a mere twelve strokes, even though her sins would normally have warranted more. She was obviously suffering a great deal more shame than normal, entirely due to the unusual and indiscreet nature of the posture. This was worth many more strokes than she was to be spared (as she later confirmed to me).

She took her beating with fortitude, unable to struggle even if she had wanted to, and was not able to stifle a few sobs or stem the flow of tears, brought about I think as much by her undignified situation as the birching itself. I dare say that the young man who had so successfully horsed his antagonist was feeling very satisfied with the outcome and the young lady's apology—that is until he remembered that it was his turn next.

In next to no time the maid, again using the second method, had the culprit hoisted with his shorts around his knees. He took his twelve stoically. For my part I found it almost effortlessly easy to deliver the strokes accurately just where they were needed, due to the elevated position of the target area.

Correlating all the data I gathered during these punishments afterwards, I listed the following observations: The recipient who is horsed high and with under garments around the knees or ankles finds struggling or kicking exceedingly difficult. In any case I should add that a compliant (or over-awed) culprit is essential All the culprits felt secure and in no danger of falling. Their concerns were entirely directed along the usual lines.

Bottoms were far more tensioned (in comparison to a culprit laying across a wooden vaulting-horse with feet touching the floor), this being due, I fancy, to the weight of the body itself; the force of gravity making it impossible to relax the seat muscles in any way. Trying to pull one's legs up succeeds in tensioning the region still further, thus increasing the pain of the punishment.

It is less important to have a big and strong horse than to use correct technique. The horse needs to bend well at the knees and take the victim high on the back—the victim's armpits should be supported by the horse's shoulders—taking a firm grip of the wrists and holding them close to the body securely. A slightly (not overdone) stooping position achieves the best stability; it also makes an excellent presentation for corporal punishment If the culprit is not held in this way it can result in undesirable pain in the arms of the victim which may interfere with the smooth execution of the punishment. It may even lead to back injury for the unfortunate horse! There is also the possibility that the horse may let the "rider" slip at the wrong moment, making it possible for the corrector to deliver an inaccurate stroke.

In conclusion therefore, I may say I have completely reversed my earlier opinion. Given the availability of a suitable horse and the room to use one effectively I will most definitely use this method again with the young gentlemen and ladies placed in my care—whenever they deserve it!

This art lovers' puzzle has a strongly mediæval flavour. All three of the illustrations originate in this period of history, and two of them are the work of Old Masters.

1. Name the painter and, if possible, the picture. 2. Name the etcher. 3. Of which famous school is this the original crest? *(The motto means "He who spares the rod, spoils the child").*

1. Pieter Brueghel the Elder *The Ass in School*. 2. Hans Holbein 3. Leith Grammar School

The Ideal Rôle for a Gentleman

The re-institution of honourable servitude is the key to a successful re-birth of Matriarchy, argues MINOS.

ISSUE 4

IT IS EXTRAORDINARY that although the servant class has existed since earliest times, today most of us are embarrassed by it. The philosophy is that servants are unnecessary; they have been abolished in the name of "democracy" and labour saving devices.

The many arguments against this will be known to readers of *The Governess*, but it reminds us of how extensive a restoration is needed to recreate a harmonious and contented society; one to replace the divided, ignorant and destructive mob of our day—a servant class which is not abolished, but simply unemployed, unhappy and directionless.

The acquiring, training and treatment of servants is particularly important to the principles of matriarchal discipline. How ludicrous is the picture of the Governess running her own errands, cleaning her rooms and dishes, or polishing her own shoes! A machine cannot perform these tasks. Neither is the employment of servants merely a matter of necessity. The relationship of mistress and servant forms two halves of one religious whole and is at the root of human contentment.

The decades during which servants have apparently become extinct have also been the most violent, unhappy, and poverty-stricken among what used to be called "the servant class" and which we now term "the masses" or, irony of ironies, "the people". The problem of how to acquire and train servants can seem so difficult that those who require them, abandon the search; and those who would achieve fulfilment as servants give up hope of it. In the honesty of the world of *The Governess*, however, it is likely to be obvious from any social encounter who should be mistress and who should serve. It is also in the tradition of *The Governess*, which is the ancient tradition of matriarchy (e.g. in Marie Antoinette's article Feminae Amez Verite **[see page 39]**, that husbands should serve their wives, or perhaps serve in female communities.

The practical difficulty, though, is how to reinstate the centuries of instilled behaviour and training for servants.

What are the models?

Older communities were smaller. The village contained a visible hierarchy, and so did the particular household. Village schools and orphanages were dedicated to the training of useful servants so that the principles were learned at an early age. (A glance at present day dole queues or of children sleeping in cardboard boxes demonstrates what a more "caring" society, as the cliché has it, that was). On leaving school, servants "belonged"—the often expressed, heartfelt desire of their great grandchildren!

Today, those older principles, when rediscovered, appear revolutionary. For example, the very word "servile" is abhorrent to the modern mind. Yet it merely means behaviour appropriate to a servant. A graciousness, now forgotten, is also involved—a recognition of mutual harmony between Mistress and servant, and of their necessity to one another. But, of course, a self respecting servant would be demeaned by showing servility to one who was not worthy of it.

We have become so used to the treadmill of payment by the hour for labour we do not enjoy, that the notion of vocation in menial tasks seems foreign. It does not strike us that to measure service in terms of payment is what is degrading—making, literally, "wage slaves" of us. The result is that the notion of the "loyal servant" has almost disappeared from our vocabulary.

It is noticeable that in earliest days servants were more often physically punished. It was replaced with the strictness over appearances detailed by Mrs Beeton and in handbooks of etiquette, published until finer lifestyles ceased circa the nineteen-thirties. Both are important, and linked, but physical discipline being so well covered by *The Governess*, I will not deal with it here.

The servant's uniform is in itself disciplinary, rendering it impossible for its wearer not to be respectful and biddable. As an aid towards humbling, the servant should be expected to take immaculate care of it. For either sex, tradition shows us that it should be trim, modestly coloured (usually black and white, green or blue) and all enclosing—all of which connote discipline. Country houses often followed the excellent practice of an outdoor uniform, usually an identifying black cloak for all servants. It should in all circumstances include that traditional badge of the servant, a starched apron (not one of the bedraggled "pinnies" worn by most waitresses these days!), and for either male or female servant to appear in a stained, bedraggled, or haphazardly fastened apron should be punished with severity.

Where the institution of domestic service is a vocation, the uniform should be worn at all times. In any case, a properly indoctrinated servant would feel uncomfortable otherwise, even in his or her own room; the appearance and regularity of correct dress marks the degree to which service is a joy and vocation. It is then an intimate, deeply satisfying, ritualised and graceful relationship that can give a lifetime's meaning between Mistress and maid or manservant.

Within Matriarchy, it is also the ideal relationship between wife and husband. A husband may be the best servant of all because his loyalty is, literally, based upon devotion. More often than most people realise, I believe that this grows naturally as the basis of a marriage, at least to a degree.

It will probably prove necessary to deny physical contact to the husband, but this does not preclude the Mistress taking lovers in time honoured Matriarchal fashion, and, provided steps are taken to prevent the odious practice of "self-abuse", the husband's drive will go unreservedly into the service of his Mistress and he will be the better and happier servant for it. It does not prevent the other shared pleasures of marriage, although it probably does require the counterbalance of even greater strictness. For example, such a husband should most certainly never be without a uniform, and more careful attention needs to be given to ways of showing respect, to punishment, to inspection of work, and to orderly timetables, than might be necessary in a less emotionally involved relationship. ✤

SEEN TO BE DONE

The solution for many of the ills of society may be found in a return to older, more shamefully effective punitive procedures, thinks AYESHA

SOMETHING SEEMS to have been overlooked during the "civilisation" of our present day system of justice. It seems two essential ingredients of punishment have fallen into disuse: Shame, and Pain.

The purpose of punishment should be corrective. It should be capable of providing the recipient with a salutary reminder not to repeat his unsociable behaviour, and also to have some deterrent value.

Upbringing in the animal kingdom, devoid of any exterior influence, has always used such methods. The lioness may cuff (or even urinate upon) an unruly cub, thus bringing it to order in the swiftest possible way.

Roman Law—the basis of all modern law—included as penalties both flagellation and exposure of the convicted (even the whipping itself) to the public. Such punishment satisfied two essential components that ensured the incident was engraved on the mind of the offender—Pain and Shame—and Justice was not only done, it was seen to be done.

Today, if someone is seriously offended (physically abused, their property destroyed) it is natural for them to expect the offender (if caught) to suffer at least as much as they have; and that the punishment will act as a deterrent to discourage that person from repeating the offence. Putting them on probation—or even locking them away—hardly represents a deterrent, especially where the conditions of their punishment are such that their daily needs are met without any effort, while the victim may well have to tolerate far less sympathetic conditions.

Proliferation of anti-social acts are the consequence of lack of discipline during upbringing. Bad behaviour has to be nipped in the bud! The earlier corrective action is applied and the more memorable it is, the more effective it will be. So corrections during formative years are particularly important. It is part of the natural development of any individual to "test the system"; if he (or she) learns to get away with it, that behaviour will be repeated, may even develop. Memorable correction is essential.

There can be few in this Society (and in society at large, I dare say) who were not aware of the value of corporal punishment, when this was permitted in our schools. Gross over-reaction to isolated cases of abuse has resulted in the situation whereby any parent who (justifiably) smacks her child may find herself arrested and charged with inflicting actual bodily harm!

Corporal punishment does not have to be brutal, and certainly not permanently damaging, to be effective. The circumstances under which it is applied are as important as its severity; for circumstance can enhance the memory of the occasion.

In the past, many conditions have been used to satisfy the conditions of Pain and Shame (public whipping, the stocks, pillory, "scold's bridle", etc.) All these satisfied the requirement for Justice to be seen to be done. However, it may well be that their discontinuance was due to these methods being so effective as deterrents that they were no longer considered necessary!

On our television screens we witness daily violent scenes of wanton anti-social activity, yet we never see any effective retribution perpetrated upon the offenders. Is this Justice? Are our sensibilities so delicate that we may see bruised and bleeding victims—but never the commensurate punishment for such deeds?

Until a few years ago the Isle of Man retained the Birch, particularly for hooliganism—and it worked! These offences were rare and those who might commit them stayed away. Now the lager louts and vandals have invaded in force. The moral, to Manx people, is obvious.

As mentioned previously, the conditions under which corporal punishment is applied are important. In the Isle of Man, it was carried out at a police station. This was wrong. It should not be left to the Police to administer; their duty is to bring offenders to Justice, not to punish. Possibly a special division of the Prison Service could be set up for the purpose, with suitable premises. Such units could be equipped with those items (or their modern equivalents) which existed in the past: the whipping-stool (or bench) on which the offender could be strapped down. Necessary or not, restraint adds to the trauma of the occasion; it also holds him in position, preventing accidental damage and ensuring the strokes land on the "seat of learning". Judicial punishments could also be videotaped (as are some police interviews) to guard against excess or abuse.

One ponders the possibility of showing some of these tapes on a special late night TV channel! Justice would be seen to be done with a vengeance, and the deterrent effect would be considerable.

Corporal punishment is ideally applied to bared buttocks, but this raises the dread demon of "modesty" (though why a delinquent's feeling should be spared in this way is not immediately obvious to me).

Although such indignity adds to the effectiveness of the punishment, there are those who believe—sincerely, no doubt—that this exposure is unacceptable, particularly (Lord knows why) in the case of females. Such objections may be overcome by the use of specially designed garments (tight-fitting "whipping drawers") which provide cover without reducing the transmission of pain sensation.

On bare flesh, a paddle, tawse or broad strap is a safer instrument for general use than cane or birch. These make an impressive noise and can be used for prolonged chastisements to great effect. While the cane is an effective instrument, in unskilled hands and on bare flesh, it can wound.

Contrary to the belief of many, wounding does not mean increased pain. It may delay recovery, or curtail the punishment. A suitable covering can prevent wounding while actually increasing the pain. In Singapore, before World War II, summary caning was carried out at police stations. Female subjects were provided with a thin, tight cotton skirt. Once bent over a table-edge, and held down by two officers, the administratrix would "wet-down" the taut fabric of the seat. This had the effect of increasing the transmission of the strokes, while (usually) preventing the skin from being broken. Six strokes with a rattan, delivered by a hefty matron, was a lesson never to be forgotten! Corporal punishment, both as a corrective measure and as a deterrent, is an essential tool and we have only to look at the effect of its withdrawal on the behaviour of the emerging generation to be aware of this.

We should not deny the use of something merely because it can be abused. Try suggesting the banning of the motor car! More innocents are injured by its misuse than ever by a good application of the Rod. But we live in a world where most commonsense values have been inverted. The Great and the Good have a good deal to answer for. ✤

FROM THE ARCHIVES

An American magazine advertisement of the 1880s. One very much doubts if such a theme could be used today!

FROM THE ARCHIVES

Did Miss Kerr-Sutherland read this? She would have been 15 at the time it was first published.

AT FOURTEEN YEARS of age I was about as good a specimen of a spoilt child as can ever be found among the present generation of children. The only son of a wealthy planter, surrounded by slaves, I had grown up ignorant of any will but my own. My father's death placed me under the guardianship of an aunt, who entered me with the least possible delay in a school of some note in Southern Louisiana...

Very few days passed before by disobedience to the governess of my class I had earned the privilege of a private interview with madam. I had already become quite aware of the fact that disobedient children in that establishment were whipped, but even when summoned to madam's room it never entered my mind that anyone would dare, or, daring, be able, to take such a liberty with me. Judge therefore, my astonishment, indignation and fury when, after a very brief struggle with two maid-servants, I found myself stripped to the shirt, fastened face downwards to the sofa. Madam having issued her orders, remained an apparently unconcerned spectator indifferent to my cries, but the use of certain words, which I had been in the habit of applying to offending servants at home, brought upon me the further inconvenience of having a kerchief tied over my mouth. Madam waited till I lay quite exhausted with the vain efforts to free myself, and then with great deliberation began to lecture me on my evil deeds, especially that culminating one, resistance to her chastisement. "For this, my child, you will receive twenty strokes with this rod." She placed the long slender bundle of twigs almost under my nose. Again I fought and kicked, but to no purpose. When I had convinced myself of the futility of all resistance, madam proceeded with the same deliberation with the punishment. It needed but very few strokes to reduce me to the frame of mind she desired. Not heeding my cries or petitions for mercy she went to the end. Unfastened from the sofa I now knelt before her, and with the greatest readiness obeyed her slightest command. The repetition of a certain formula used on such occasions, acknowledging the fault and thanking madam for the punishment, kissing the rod and finally madam's hand seemed to come quite natural. But a much severer test of that new born obedience followed, when I was dressed in the costume of a child three or four years old—drawers, petticoats, short dress, all beautifully embroidered and ornamented, and placed by madam in the Kindergarten class. Of course, it is extremely humiliating for a big boy to be dressed like a little girl, to be made to play with little children, to have to repeat their infantile lessons, to be put to bed at seven o'clock, and, worst of all, to have to submit to a great deal of teasing from the older girls, who delighted in making me carry a doll, and submitting to other indignities; but all aided in producing the one effect desired—prompt obedience to all in authority.

I was restored to my place in the boy's class and allowed to resume the ordinary dress. I remained a considerable time under madam's charge, but never again incurred punishment for direct disobedience, though like the rest, boys and girls big and little, received punishment for minor offences. This, madam, having placed the culprit across her knee, after letting down trousers or drawers, administered with a short rod.

Madam's influence over her pupils was unbounded and lasting. I thoroughly believe, were she to confront any of them to-day, grown men or women, those well-remembered words, "My child, again have you been disobedient; bring me the rod, take off, etc. etc." would be received with unhesitating obedience.

JOHN E.C.H.
14th March, 1885, *Town Talk*

The Queen of Rods and the Young Gentleman

An Exquisite and Meticulous Tutorial in the Proper Use of the Birch

By CAMPANIA

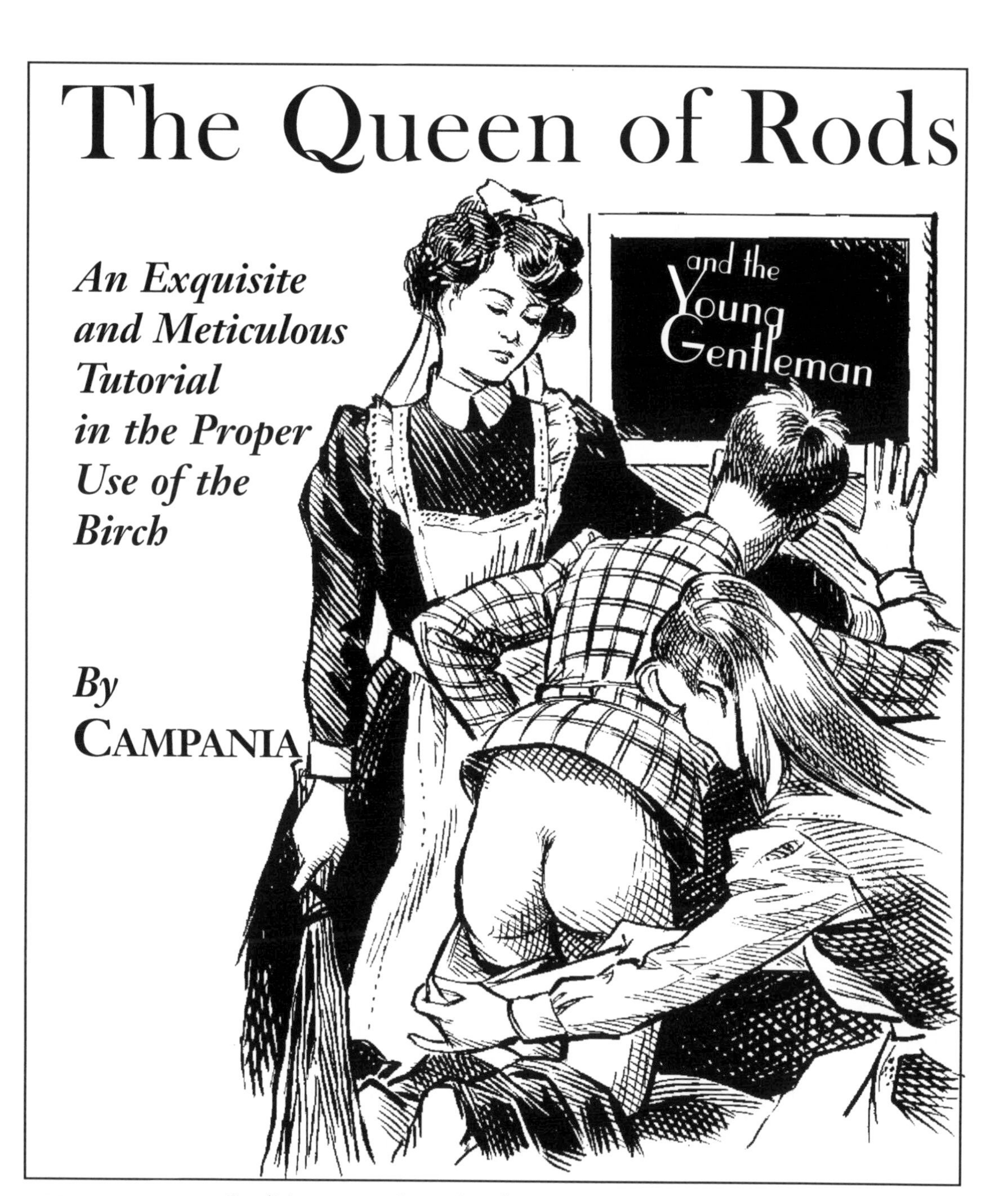

IN ANSWER TO Cerdic's queries about the use of the birch **[see page 9]**, *The Governess* was right to point out that it is comparatively cheap to make. The fact that its preparation is time consuming and some care and attention must be given to its preservation are not disadvantages. These features add considerably to the instrument's undoubted mystique and help to keep it as feared as it deserves to be. The birch requires that the disciplinarian, and for best results possibly the recipient too, should fully understand its use. Such understanding requires consideration of history, physiology, psychology and indeed simple mechanics. In an effort to improve Cerdic's education (and possibly that of some Members) I offer the following observations.

Firstly, note that there is a spectrum of pain, ranging from the sharp to the broad, which may be termed its acuity as distinct from its force or severity. As a guide, a thin cane produces a sharp, more acute, pain while a rigid paddle gives a broad, less acute, one. I assume that Associate Members will be well acquainted with the distinction while any disciplinarian who is not would be well advised to consider the need to base her practice of discipline on personal experience of the effects. The birch, if correctly constructed, is almost certainly the most acute of instruments.

It is my belief that the more muscular bottoms of young men are better able to withstand the broader sorts of pain which thus makes the sharper particularly appropriate for their discipline in serious cases. Such pain is produced by thin and flexible instruments. The birch tree has the property of producing comparatively long, very slender and whippy twigs to which, by the good offices of nature, it adds the extra weight of buds at precisely the time of year when the behaviour of the young male is at its most exuberant and in need of discipline.

THE BIRCH is the traditional instrument of punishment in England and many other European countries. In former times the Dame of every village school would keep one close to hand to enliven the learning of her young charges and a privately employed Governess would ensure that a supply was readily available within the house to be sent for when needed. For them, the birch was traditionally constructed from a number of flexible twigs bound together to form a handle and which branched out at the operating end into a "bush" consisting of a large number of very, very thin, extremely supple and stinging twiglets. In this form it might vary from the very short, intended to be used, usually on younger boys, in the over-the-knee position, to four or five feet in length requiring a considerable swing. In the latter case the "bush" of birch might be affixed to a rigid handle.

Unfortunately, in male-dominated schools and for judicial use, the birch became a brutal bundle of fairly thick branches which in some cases were not birch at all. We shall confine our attention to the more subtle and feminine instrument of tradition.

Since it requires that a young man's trousers and underpants be taken down, and since the thin twigs do not inflict great severity at a single stroke, this is not an instrument for hurried use. When trade with the east was established it quickly became apparent that rattan provided excellent instruments for more immediate punishment and the use of the birch became confined to dealing with more serious offences for which time and ceremony were appropriate. This reservation of use has certainly helped to endow the instrument with its own mystique. I am not convinced that it counts as the most severe of instruments but the particularly sharp nature of its pain together with the associated ritual can inflict very effective punishment.

Let us consider then the use of the birch on a young man whom we may call "Cerdic".

There is no need to dwell on the usual preliminaries to discipline except to say that, if this is to be Cerdic's first birching, it will be necessary to explain what is involved in, to him, painful detail and he may be somewhat surprised to find that he will have to wait some 24 hours for his punishment

Firstly each birch must be freshly made and, for obvious reasons, a separate rod is required for each boy. Cerdic will therefore be made to prepare his own birch, collecting the twigs to specification, binding them and soaking the resulting rod overnight. Some supervision will be necessary to ensure that the most painful instrument is produced and, during the process, he will have plenty of time to speculate on the likely effect of those thin twigs across his bare buttocks.

Traditionally, birches were soaked in brine, both to intensify the sting where the skin might be broken and as an antiseptic. The latter is still necessary as the twigs are a natural and otherwise untreated product. If the rod is removed from its soaking water and treated with T.C.P. or Dettol just before use much the same effect (in both respects) can be achieved.

The soaking process, with the upper ends of the twigs temporarily bound together, is necessary to ensure that the rod will hold a comparatively confined shape when in use as well as ensuring maximum flexibility. It also means that the miscreant will spend many hours in anticipation.

For the greatest psychological effect, some 30 minutes before the scheduled time, Master Cerdic will be put to stand waiting somewhere where he can see the birch that is to be used on him while all is made ready in the punishment room.

THERE ARE two traditional positions for birching: hoisting and the block. Hoisting or horsing requires the assistance of a strong young woman who will have to support the miscreant without moving, a difficult task if the birching is to go on for some time as perhaps it needs to. The Return of the Classroom Horse **[pp. 43-48]** gives an very full description of this method, its difficulties and the advantages it offers when it is rendered possible. Authentic blocks, on the other hand, are rarely available and, from what I have seen of the usual design, may be too low. I therefore recommend something similar to a gymnastic horse with a kneeling stool placed before it. I shall refer to this as a "block" to avoid confusion with the human horse. This block will need to be at the right height to present Cerdic's buttocks at about the level of his mistress' waist or slightly above, with the stool being suitable for him to lie comfortably across the block.

To make Cerdic's punishment more effective—both for himself and others—the process should be witnessed by fellow pupils, both male and female. I will assume that this is possible; adjustments can be made to the ritual if not.

The pupils are lined up and marched into the punishment room and, when all is ready, Cerdic, bearing his birch, is brought in. After handing the rod to the Mistress with appropriate words requesting a thorough whipping, he steps over to the stool and places his hands on his head. An assistant called the "holder" (who may be a maid, assistant mistress or fellow pupil) then unfastens and pulls down Cerdic's trousers and underpants. The boy then kneels on the stool and lies forward over the block while the holder, standing at the miscreant's head, pulls up his shirt exposing the bare bottom for all to see, and remains there with her hands on his back, her duty being principally to keep the shirt up as holding down as such is not usually required. The Mistress flicks the last few drops of water from the birch and takes her position. If a particular number of strokes has been prescribed, a fourth participant may be required to count the strokes aloud. They are delivered with pronounced pauses between them. The mass of thin twigs ensures that the whole surface of the buttocks is thoroughly chastised and they inevitably reach parts which other instruments do not.

Mistresses should note that great care is

needed when birching. An expert caner will not need to be told that she must stand well round to the culprit's left (assuming she is right-handed), so that the right buttock is invisible, and to aim for the part of the birch about nine inches from the end to land on the left buttock (that measurement needs to be adjusted to suit the size of Cerdic's bottom, of course). She must, however, be more careful than with the comparatively rigid cane not to stand too close or the ends of the twigs will wrap round the boy's body. Though a young man should be made to keep his knees slightly apart, so that the twigs do indeed reach all parts of the buttocks, the careful mistress should ensure that they are not spread too much for, although her pupil has no right to modesty or dignity, he does have a right to expect the sort of skill in which chastisement is confined to the bottom cheeks or the very tops of the legs. (A young woman being birched should be instructed to keep her knees together. Members will fully understand the reason for this.) For the same reason the mistress must ensure that the upper part of the birch is bound into as tight a bundle as possible while soaking.

There are three sorts of stroke of which only two should be used by the considerate disciplinarian. In the so-called stopper the mistress stops the birch in the position in which it lands on the buttocks. The bouncer requires a flick of the wrist to get it to bounce up after impact thereby, scientists claim, transferring double the amount of momentum to the recipient's hind quarters. Be very careful about any sort of follow through, this can easily lead to the undesirable cutter stroke in which the birch twigs are drawn across the punished flesh breaking the skin. This is merely damaging rather than painful.

But to return to Master Cerdic. He was probably quite surprised at the first stroke; not at its severity but at how sharp the pain was. As the birch slowly and repeatedly swishes down, his buttocks become covered with patterns of fine and intersecting weals and he feels the sting build-up in intensity. There is little point in administering a mere six strokes with this instrument; and experience would indicate that Cerdic will get the most benefit from a minimum of eighteen. Possibly his mistress will not have announced the number in advance, preferring instead to birch on and on until his gasps vocalise into yells. Will there be tears? I hope so.

The holder may be given a final duty of wiping Cerdic's buttocks with a towel—carefully, for it will be very tender—to remove moisture and particles of birch before he attempts to dress.

Many mistresses will require that when Cerdic stands up after punishment he express his humble thanks. The more considerate will note, however, that, if she has done her job well, he may be in no condition to do this immediately and she will allow the expressions of gratitude to be postponed until later. I would not normally expect the recently punished to sweep the punishment room either, for the same reason. This is a job for other pupils or, in the absence of any such, the Mistress should regard it as a duty which enables her to share more fully the experience of the culprit. If the birch has been thoroughly soaked it will not splinter overmuch and the task should not be an arduous one.

As I have already said, the birch lacks the physical severity of some other instruments but nevertheless, correctly applied and with due ceremony, a birching binds Mistress and Pupil together in a cathartic experience, partners, rather than antagonists, in a powerfully deep disciplinary process. At the very least, young Cerdic will have experienced a humiliating and psychologically effective punishment which he will not want to repeat in a hurry.

SMACKING AS A REWARD

***The standard corporal reaction is not necessarily a penalty, argues* GODIVA.**

WHEN CHILD CARE workers warn you against smacking your children, they tend to adopt one of two attitudes. Either your teenage children will become stronger than you and beat you up, or else your kids are trying to provoke a response and when you smack them "they've won". Both are ridiculous. I know one six-foot chap with a Brown Belt in Judo who was seriously told he should fear a thirteen-year-old boy. The other story is really an indictment of the storyteller. Her children are unwanted pets, and the only way they can get her to take any notice of them is to cause trouble. Her strategy of ignoring them is far more cruel than smacking, and it's actually an excuse for continuing with her customary indifference.

With all the fuss about child abuse, we tend to forget how acceptable corporal punishment was until very recently. It was a weekly feature in children's comics, like the *Beano* and the *Dandy*. Characters like Dennis The Menace are still with us, being naughty in various strange ways and coming unstuck as a result. Nowadays Dennis suffers some strange fates in the last picture, but back in the 1960's he'd be shown getting his bottom spanked. His female equivalents, Beryl The Peril and Minnie The Minx, would get spanked too. Nobody objected, either adult or child, because in a sense the spanking was a happy ending, a kind of consummation of the parent-child relationship.

According to Desmond Morris (the behaviourist), spanking is a natural behaviour pattern we inherited from the apes. The bending over originated from the female mating posture, in which the female ape presents her rump to the male as an invitation to mount. This rump-presentation posture evolved into a general submission signal, because the submissive animal in a conflict situation usually signals his status by a display of harmlessness, imitating a young animal or a female. In apes as in humans, either sex may submit to either sex in this fashion. In humans, though, a more punitive behaviour pattern has evolved.

It may seem strange that any adult would choose to assume a submissive rôle. Dennis The Menace can help us here, or maybe Judge Dredd. Teenagers actually enjoy Judge Dredd being tough on delinquents. As children, we don't necessarily want to be allowed to get away with everything. If we did, the result would be a tremendous feeling of insecurity. In a sense, smacking is indeed a reward, because it indicates the parent's commitment to caring; and adults can play at being children, as children play at being adults. Look at some young couples. It's probably a rehearsal for having babies.

Apart from my own feelings, I discovered this while participating in an informal Therapy Group. Inevitably, we started as an all female group without any leadership. However, men did turn up, especially after the word got round that some of us, being leftovers from the 1960s, had tried sessions with group nudity. The mixed sessions weren't always successful. Certain individuals of both sexes tended to be inconsiderate towards other group members, some of whom had very real emotional problems. So we invented a system of forfeits for misbehaviour, jokingly at first, on the lines of school punishment, with ritualised spanking being one example. This quickly got rid of some of the men, because although the women couldn't force them to submit to this forfeit, our friend the Judo Brown Belt easily could, and did.

What surprised us then was the attitude of the remaining men. Not only were they prepared to play the game of forfeits, they confessed to the strange feeling that it would actually be appropriate for them to be beaten occasionally, though they couldn't give any reason for their feelings. Full of curiosity, we started to explore this question in depth. The sessions got rather intimate and occasionally embarrassing, and some of the less understanding women left the group too. At this point I should say that although various people received corporal punishment, often in a group setting and not entirely clothed, we weren't running a flagellant brothel or anything approaching that.

Various points emerged from our experiments.

The most important part of a disciplinary session, surely, is the emotional state of the main participants, and any audience (if there is one). This is particularly true if anything like pain is involved, because only a more intense emotional state can enable you to discount any painful sensation and get a meaningful experience from the punishment. And, strangely in the circumstances, you become far more sensitive to other people's attitudes to what's going on. Obviously nobody is going to receive a caning when most of the people present find the whole thing distasteful, but it's more subtle than that. You sense as soon as anybody feels the slightest bit negative, and then the whole scenario has to be called off. It's rather like the Spiritualist medium who can't perform while bad vibrations are present.

My own one-to-one sessions evolved from this practical consideration. It's easier to get the required empathy when only two people are involved, and one of the most important factors in both counselling and discipline is setting up the necessary confidence and fellow feeling between the participants. It seems to me that when a man bends over and bares his buttocks for me, he's decided that he needs to revert to childhood, probably for therapeutic reasons. It's quite flattering for me to know I'm a suitable person to trust with these feelings. Also, it's this mutual feeling which enables the man to receive pain when necessary, and experience it primarily, as a shared event. Like most women, I'm attracted to the shape of a man's buttocks, and I feel that any attention I pay to them should be a gesture of caring and friendship. It seems strange that pain, or at least discomfort, can be experienced this way, but obviously this is possible, indeed essential for many males once they've summoned up the courage to admit it. The gratification I get is the result of being with the man while he undergoes the ordeal willingly at my hands, and feels the same way about it as I do.

Obviously my one-to-one sessions can be more intimate than any group activity. I certainly prefer to use the cane on the man's bare skin, so that I can see the effect in terms of any marks which result.

At this point I'll admit that I do like to see the man's buttocks acquiring a collection of stripes, but this isn't actually "sadism". I'm actually submissive in my attitude to men, but for me there's something magical in seeing my Lord and Master submitting willingly in his turn. Also it's a safety measure to be able to see the marks, and distribute them evenly so that no injury is inflicted. A severe caning will result in red weals, but these fade away over the following week or two, and no damage is done. I might massage his buttocks afterwards, and I'm often impressed by the lumpy feel of the skin and the hotness of his behind, presumably because the blood is circulated more to that area. Again, it's not sadism on my part, but a feeling of gladness that the man has endured this effect willingly, at my best.

Some men enjoy inspecting their stripes in the mirror, and I can see they're quite proud of them. At least one man said that he felt as if he was a sort of domesticated animal who belonged to me. He felt as if I'd in a sense put my brand on him to show he was my property, and he felt proud to carry the marks on his rump for that reason. At any rate, a caning can be an emotionally rewarding experience, and they're glad to have the stripes to remember it by for a while.

As you may have guessed, most members of my Therapy Group are unmarried, or at least unattached. But there are married men too, and their wives have obviously wondered where the stripes came from. It can be upsetting for them, because fresh weals can look like quite an injury, especially with swelling and grazing.

Naturally their first reaction has often been to view me as a prostitute, and strangely this arouses less resentment than a love-affair would. Usually I've managed to establish a dialogue with the wife, and once she understands I'm basically giving counselling about feelings which her husband and I both have in common, things seem to resolve themselves.

Not all wives understand the need for corporal punishment, but often they're glad to have the issue taken off their hands, once they realise I've got a life of my own and I'm not aiming to steal their chap. I have had wives who stayed to witness the caning, maybe out of curiosity, maybe to supervise things, and it seemed to me they had a very constructive attitude.

In general I'd say the wives were very loyal and understanding, and if they didn't want to get involved in disciplinary activity, they accepted that I could fill the gap and it would stop their chap looking for another partner.

Finally, I should add that the need for discipline comes to an end if I've done my job properly. Having been satisfactorily punished, the man's Unconscious is pacified, and his instincts sort themselves out. Probably he still needs an occasional beating, but there's nothing worrying or desperate about it, and it can be accepted as a part of life and not an embarrassing problem. And surely this is the ultimate reward for being brave enough to accept the discipline when required. ✤

GENERAL FEATURES

BOOK REVIEWS

POETRY

1993

NEW LIGHT ON MISS KERR-SUTHERLAND'S LATER CAREER

The Memoirs of the late Contessa d'Asti e Piemonte prove a connexion with Italy of the early '30s.

Research by Candida

In the Publisher's Introduction to *A Guide To The Correction Of Young Gentlemen* it is stated that on her release from prison in 1925 (?), Miss Alice Kerr-Sutherland "emigrated to the Dominion of South Africa". This supposition—which the Publisher now admits was based upon rather sketchy premises—has recently, and conclusively, been shewn to be partially incorrect; and a deal more light has been shed upon the later life and career of the great lady in whose honour our Society has been formed.

The piece of evidence to which we refer is a book called *Roma Nova: Italy under the Duce*, written by Teodora di Santangelo (or Sant' Angelo), as she still was at the time of writing, later La Contessa d'Asti e Piemonte, wife of that Conde who was Italy's Deputy Ambassador to the United Nations from 1953–55 (and was later killed in his Maserati during the last of the famous Mille Miglia races to be held, in 1957). The book was published in the United States (by Jonathan Meale Inc., Boston, in 1952), but such was the public perception of fascism at that time—even the relatively unmalevolent form represented by Mussolini—that it was never, we understand, widely distributed and no British Commonwealth publishing rights were negotiated at all. We owe our possession of the relevant photocopy of this vitally interesting book to the generosity of one of our first Full Members, who asks that we refer to her only by her *nom-de-fouet* of Geneviève (which we should naturally have done in any case). Our deepest thanks to her.

The authoress and her younger sister Maria Pia were the two daughters of a notable Italian banker who, despite having built a successful career in the United States as a financial consultant during the pre-Crash '20s, had felt the romantic call of the New Italy which Mussolini was forging and had returned with his family to put his expertise and connexions at the disposal of the state. Both girls had been born in the United States and reared in a well-to-do Lakenhurst home, according to the vaguely "liberal" precepts then beginning to take hold in some circles of American life. On their return to Italy, however, their life changed in more ways than one. The New Order then taking popular hold in Italy, while having little of the harshness of the Prussian style of Cæsarism which was later partly modelled upon it, nonetheless exalted the sterner, more heroic standards of Ancient Rome (a society in which children had been strictly disciplined, for their own

Is this the face of Alice?

Tamara de Lempicka's portrait of "The Mature Woman", circa 1930. Subject unknown.

most schools. Less than one year after re-emigration to Italy, and dissatisfied with his daughters' behaviour (an outrageous incident at a matinée given by their mother is described by the authoress in distinctly unrepentant tones), their father engaged a British governess to take them in hand. It was an inauspicious meeting.

My first impressions of the new visitor were mixed. The first thing one noticed about her was her aura of great vitality. She was one of those people who seem to live on a plane of greater intensity than most of us. In our house this was less remarkable than it might have been

benefit and that of the Republic). For example, boys were forbidden by many regional ordinances to wear long trousers until they were 16; and corporal punishment was used in elsewhere, for we were used to a succession of vital, witty, clever and often eccentric visitors. Beside this great vitality, and almost seeming to contradict it, was a certain severity, or starchiness, which we [the authoress and her younger sister] at first took to be a pose or some form of sophisticated play-acting, but which we quickly discovered to be wholly genuine…

We were precocious children. We sat at dinner with the grown-ups and joined in every sort of conversation… our mode of life was about as far removed from the life of a Victorian nursery as could well be imagined. We were (I think I may say without immodesty at this distance of time) clever, amusing and very much above ourselves. Our visitor, while (I believe) appreciating our better qualities, seemed in some respects openly to disapprove of us, or our conduct. It was an entirely novel experience. Most guests either liked us or ignored us. Disapproval was simply not a thing we had experienced or were able to comprehend, and it was oddly disturbing. [P. 35.]

Throughout, the authoress refers to the new governess as "Miss Carr Sutherland". "Carr" is a traditional alternative pronunciation of the (Scottish) cognomen Kerr, and may therefore indicate how the lady herself pronounced her name (since we can be sure that she would have instructed her pupils how to say it correctly). Tantalisingly, there are no real descriptions of her régime. One would have been particularly interested in this since in her immortal book she refers, albeit obliquely, to the corporal discipline of schoolgirls.

On page 47 there are two highly relevant passages:

Of the English social order as it then was [Miss Kerr-Sutherland] was severely critical. It would be easy to suggest that she had been soured by her experiences in her own country (I did not learn the nature of these until many some years afterwards, and did not fully understand them when first I heard them). For my part I find this interpretation rather insulting to her intelligence. She felt, I think objectively, that the contemporary state of affairs [in England], unless some ordering principle or spiritual direction could be found, must lead to a state of social degeneracy and moral anarchy…

From this, and from her presence in a well-to-do Italian household at this particular period of history, it is reasonable to deduce that, like the fictional Miss Jean Brodie, Miss Kerr Sutherland was romantically attracted to the values then being promulgated by fascisti intellectuals. It is easy to forget that, in those days (the late 20s and early 30s), fascism was regarded by many of the best and bravest as an heroic, spartan and above all noble ideal. Its later associations of race hatred and systematic persecution were not dreamed of by the vast mass of its idealistic supporters, and in any case were the product of the (hugely debased) German version, which came along afterwards.

Before coming to us Miss Carr Sutherland had lived for several years in Paris. She told my sister and I many stories of the artistic and aristocratic circles displaced by the turmoil of war and revolution. It sounded to me like a curious, Bohemian existence, greatly contrasting with the life of authority and social responsibility which they had occupied before the War…

She was at some time a friend of Tamara de Lempicka… [who] had painted her portrait.

Here, perhaps, is another reason for her return to her original profession. The European circles in which she had latterly moved may have been vital and amusing, appealing possibly to the theatrical side of her nature, but one may imagine that she also found in them, after a time, something rather vapid and unsatisfying, while their loose moral tone may not have sat well either with her English sense of decorum or her austere Scottish sensibility.

But if the connexion with Tamara de Lempicka be true, it is news indeed. Madame de Lempicka was perhaps the greatest of pure Art Deco painters, and she too had moved in the circles of the mighty and influential during the turbulent years of the later 20s and early 30s. If she ever painted a portrait of Alice Kerr-Sutherland, however, it is impossible to say, since no mention of such a work is anywhere to be found. Perhaps it languishes to this day in a private collection; perhaps it did not survive the Second World War, or perhaps, like the famous projected portrait of Gabrielle d'Annunzio, it was never actually painted.

If it was, we may fervently hope that it some day comes to light, as Madame de Lempicka's pure, sensual, neo-traditional, stylised manner would surely have captured the essence of the great disciplinarienne in the most breathtakingly poignant manner.

Be that as it may, after three and one-half years in the service of the di Santangelo family of Rome, the by now elderly governess departed to return to England. However she left behind her a deep and abiding impression in the mind of this particular adolescent girl.

> I have sometimes wondered why she did return to England. Her life in Europe seemed to suit her admirably… But after all, she was an English [sic] governess; her roots were deep in her native soil. (P.55.)

Or perhaps she sensed the pending European calamity and wished, as is only natural, to be with her "ain folk"?

Any general analysis of this extra information about Miss Kerr-Sutherland's life must acknowledge that it raises more questions than it solves, especially since the authoress does not always supply the relevant dates. We know, however, that she (that is, the authoress) was ten years old when the family re-emigrated to Italy, and as she was herself born "during the first full year of peace" (1919–20) it must have been in the year 1929–30 that Miss Kerr-Sutherland was engaged by Salvatore di Santangelo to take charge of his daughters' upbringing. Since she was herself born in 1870, she must at the time have been in her sixtieth year, which is (and was) a very distinguished age at which to be moving in important European political and social circles. It is also strange, to say the least, that a mere children's governess should have been welcome in such exalted society. The only possible explanation is that her real occupation—and presumably the reason for her *notoriété*—was well known to the wealthy and titled emigré community of post-war Paris. Did she discipline those of its members who required this service of her? One may certainly hope so.

There remains the South African evidence. A death certificate in her name was certainly issued by the Cape Town registrar on October 30th, 1939 [if any of our members has connexions in South Africa and is willing to undertake a little research it might be possible to locate her grave].

According to *Roma Nova*, she left Italy in about 1933–34, in order to return to Great Britain. Did she emigrate to the faraway Dominion soon afterwards? We cannot say; and the remainder of her life is shrouded in mystery. ✤

THE QUEEN OF RODS &

How To Make A Birch-Rod

A PROPERLY MADE birch-rod is an instrument of surpassing beauty—and tragedy, since if correctly manufactured, with due regard for the age, sex and physique of the recipient and the gravity of the offence, and administered with finesse, it will last precisely as long as the apportioned chastisement—and not one stroke longer. Construction of the rod, therefore, must be undertaken with all these variable factors very much in mind, though a birch which outlasts the punishment for which it has been specifically created is less grievous a sin against æsthetics than one which flies apart at any earlier stage.

BEGIN BY selecting and cutting the required number of suitable twigs. Choose green (young) twigs if you wish to shew mercy; otherwise select switches from the older trees. In all cases trim off all greenery, and the lower side-shoots, from each switch, preserving the general club-like profile.

PLACE THE prepared switches on a table and take some moments to study them. Take note of the spread and direction of even the smallest side-twig, and remember that the greater number of these finer twigs that remain within the envelope of the finished rod, the more slowly will the birch move through the air; and the lighter and more diffused will be the resulting stroke. This prime characteristic can to some extent be cancelled out by the length of the finished rod, and the power behind the stroke.

HAVING GROUPED the trimmed switches into the perfect punitive profile, secure loosely with string while you prepare the handle. All birch-rods should be properly dressed with ribbon—preferably silk—before presentation and eventual use. With the ribbon, begin winding from the base upwards, relaxing the tension as you ascend; this preserves the conical shape. Bisect the free end of the ribbon and knot, then fashion into as elegant a bow as you can contrive.

Bushier Birches

THE GROWING season, the age of the tree and its location within the wood are all of great importance. For example, older trees—especially those that grow in deep shade—often produce twigs that are more sharply convoluted. These also tend to be the harder twigs, and so form longer-lasting rods. They also make bushier rods, and need more careful thinning if the air resistance is not to impede the force of the descent.

The Eton Rod

THE FAMOUS style of birch used at Eton College was traditionally made from four-foot stems of the bushier, hard-wooded type, bound tightly for at least two-thirds of their overall length, forcing the unbound twigs out into a spray rather larger than the bottom it was used to punish. Used with force, this wrought fearful results.

The Judicial Birch

AS USED by Juvenile Courts in mainland Britain until the end of World War II (and in the Channel Islands & the Isle of Man until much later), the Judicial Birch was not necessarily made from birch-wood at all—willow was often a favoured choice. The rods were up to 42 inches long and stripped of all greenery and superfluous twigs; five or seven switches of this type made a penetrating weapon. At the other end of the scale of severity, willow was also the favoured choice of the Germans for the correction of younger culprits—so-called "soap-rods" normally used in a household for frothing up the liquid soap in the bucket before laundering clothes. Willow-rods were also favoured in Ireland—true birch is not abundant in that country—where rods of this type are still called "sallies".

Types of Birch-rod

MANY TYPES of birch-rod exist—in a sense, each rod is unique, since each birch-tree is also unique, and no collection of switches will ever be the same. The most refined form of this punishment requires the culprit himself to furnish the made-up rod for his own castigation. However this requires a generous amount of the Governess's time, and may not, for many reasons, be convenient. Another factor is the unavailability of birch within urban environments. It therefore behoves the conscientious Governess to lay in supplies of birch at every opportunity. Left with their leaves on, and the bases immersed in cold water, the twigs will keep for some days. Made up into rods—that is, with all greenery stripped away—it is best to keep them almost wholly immersed in "pickle"—a weak saline or vinaigre solution. The rod should be well shaken before use. The pickle not only preserves the wood; it also hardens it to some extent and prevents early breakage during the punishment.

Some Governesses also follow the old practice of levying a charge on the pupil for the trouble she has taken in procuring the rod for his correction. At Eton in the last century this levy was half-a-guinea a "half" (term), but currency has inflated since those days and a fee of ten guineas is by no means unreasonable.

BOOK REVIEW

A Century Later, Young Ladies Catch Up

"THE SCOPE of the work is limited to the correction of female miscreants by female disciplinarians: and although much of what appears herein may be applied to the disciplining of both sexes, the differences are sufficient to make it desirable to issue a booklet specifically designated for the use of feminine institutions."

Thus part of the preamble to *The Female Disciplinary Manual*, Ministry of Education Official Pamphlet no. 442/21315/87/A/14 according to its duck-egg-blue jacket. Its nominal price (of three shillings and sixpence) and its subject matter appear to indicate a charming re-publication of some long-lost document, not at all unlike the provenance of Miss Kerr-Sutherland's own book. However the third line of the Preamble tells a different story: "In accordance with Section 52, Paragraph I(B) of the Education Act (2032)..." 2032? At last all becomes clear. This little (64 pp) book is a time traveller: by some miraculous agency it has journeyed back into our own era where it may be seen as a genuine anachronism in a unique sense of the term. It is also a work of great distinction, for many reasons.

TFDM is not a "female-version" of *A Guide to the Correction of Young Gentlemen*, though one might be excused for assuming so; and certainly there are considerable commonalities of approach and style. But there are also great differences. There is only a single illustration, for example (officially approved weights of cane), and the writing is even more compressed and lucid than Miss Kerr-Sutherland's own (admirably lucid) prose. The single greatest difference is one of refinement, expressed in many ways, the most contentious of which will surely be the rigorous disapproval of what Miss Kerr-Sutherland calls la déculottage:

Although as might be expected, each of the fundamental instruments and modes of correction is dealt with in a chapter of its own (spanking, the ruler, the switch, the birch et al), rather in the Kerr-Sutherland mode, it is clearly the Cane which, to the lady writers of this fascinating book, is the true "Queen of Rods". Nowhere else can such a degree of rattan-esoterica be found—the writers clearly possess enormous experience. Did you know, for example, that it is unnecessary to steep an entire cane in water in order to preserve it? Apparently standing the base of the instrument in water is sufficient—capillary attraction does the rest: the cane "drinks" its fill.

This is an excellent book, fully comparable to the Guide, and indeed surpassing it in intensity and sensibility. The régime it describes is uncompromising to a degree, which is not to say that there are not a great many young ladies who would be glad of a chance to experience it—and young gentlemen also. Miss Kerr-Sutherland would surely have approved.

CANDIDA

SQUIRE HARDMAN

by George Colman the Younger

[Abridged]

HAIL, GODDESS of the stern and bended brow,
Revered and worshipped, yet unnam'd till now
Ev'n in this land where Thou hast most acclaim,
And where the rites conducive to Thy fame
Have grown to be a kind of national game,
Hail, dear Domestic Discipline, the nurse
Of Albion's fame (for better or for worse)
And cast a fav'ring spell upon my verse!

AND YE, the votaries of her Deity,
Her lovely priestesses, where'er ye be,
Whether in castle, cottage, boarding school,
Nursery or workhouse, Ye that bear the rule
O'er British youth and British backsides: hail,
You strait-laced Tyrants of the head and tail!
To you I dedicate these tingling rhimes
Made for the delectation of the times,
So that they may, as other Farces do,
Amuse the public for a month or two,
Though if perchance posterity allows
Such merit in them that they still arouse
In future minds (congenial to the theme)
An int'rest in the Flagellant régime,
Pray let me pay their debt of gratitude
To One pre-eminent in the multitude
Of members of your whipping Sisterhood.

AYE, MARY Anne! ev'n Thee let me invoke
With whom I've shared the matrimonial yoke
For nigh ten years, nor ever ceas'd to find
Fresh cause for jubilation since we join'd
Our hands and fortunes, and our tastes combin'd:
To Thee, then, if these lines should live indeed
To warm the future's blood, and fill a need
For all subscribers to the Flogging Creed,
I consecrate the song; and may it find
A lasting place among those works design'd
T'erect the carnal spirits of mankind.
Now Gentle Reader, lend me first of all
Your fancy's vision—what the "Lakers" call
"The inward eye", "the bliss of solitude",
Or what else dignifies a moonstruck mood—
At any rate, pray lend me it, and gaze
On the two pictures which my poem lays
Before you (as 'twere in the Playhouse): so,
Turn down the lights, the curtain raise, and Lo!
See The Good Governess at close of day,
The supper eaten, the toys put away
The ev'ning lesson heard, the prayers said,
And her young charges all sent up to bed,
And she now reading from the little book
Wherein their daily crimes are summ'd: who took
That liberty, and who that extra jam;
Who lost his temper and let fall a d– –n
Who pull'd his little sister's hair, and lied
When tax'd with it—and so much more beside,
You see how well her patience has been tried.

Yet mark the pensive smile that steals apace
Over the features of that modest face,
That face so stern and sombre that you'd vow
'Twas downright plain, unless you saw it now!
Ah see, indeed, how the becoming blood
Tinges her neck and rises in a flood
To nurture in each cheek a lovely Rose,
See how her breath more swiftly comes and goes,
How her mouth softens and her glowing eyes
Have gain'd in brilliance and increas'd in size;
And when she rises, how her form has grown
In majesty, and in that motion shewn
A very Juno rising from her throne!
She walks, 'tis Music, and she stands, 'tis Art;
But what is this which strikes you to the heart
In yon fine pose, so graceful and so grand?
Is it the cane that quivers in her hand?
At any rate, see how the dear girl's beauty
Wakes at the prospect of her painful duty:
Smiling she turns, and softly trips upstairs;
And let that Reader follow her who dares.

I, FOR MY part, am loath to play the spy
On the good woman, and I'll tell you why.
There are some scenes, as ev'ry Author knows,
Whose power is multiplied, whose pathos grows
Through presentation by some means oblique:
E.g., Iphigenia's dying shriek
Heard off the stage—th' effect is full of power;
Or take the little Princes in the Tower,
Smother'd by hearsay: how that moves the heart!
And Sophocles' Medea shews the art
Of moving sympathy's profoundest springs
By knocking off her children—in the wings.

IMAGINE TO yourself a Guest, therefore,
In the same house, and one dividing door
Between his chamber and the children's room
A Bachelor of fortune, one to whom
Such sounds as from th' adjoining chamber come
Are music sweeter than the heavenly spheres'.
He stops, enraptured by the cries he hears,
His heart in's mouth, his whole soul in his ears:
Each whistling stroke, each howl and plea and sob
Make his blood boil, his very being throb;
For he, by taste and moral judgment both,
Favours the drastic governance of youth:

The study of the whip was, to his mind
The "properest study" of all womankind,
And woman's proper sphere—a boy's behind.
Greedier than courtier for the Royal smile
Was he for flogging in the good old style;
Welcomer than to bride her wedding bells
To him the sounds of discipline, the yells
And shrieks of a well flagellated boy.
This was his Hobby, this his greatest joy.
So, little wonder that you see him stand
Mute-motionless, his chin within his hand,
His ears upon the stretch, and in his eyes
A vision of domestic paradise;
And when you understand this tranced guest
Was still unshav'd, and only partly dress'd,
'Tis still less wonder that the jolly sinner
Should be, that ev'ning, rather late for dinner.

"The matter? Why, if you must know, my dear,
'Tis that I find her—well, much too severe.
"Severe—a fiddlestick!" my Lord exclaims:
"Whate'er her methods, I approve her aims.
Hardman, d'ye know my Billy has the names
Of all the Kings from Norman William down,
And Bob can tell an adverb from a noun!"
"And at what cost, my Lord?" his wife puts in:
"The boys are black and blue from discipline!"
"No matter. Faith, Miss Lashley's in the right.
I never knew the boys half so polite:
Even little Oliver, who's only three—"
"—She takes him every night across her knee!"
"But Joan, the French and Latin that she's
taught him—"
"—Granted, my dear, but have you seen
his b – – m?"

And there, *dear Reader, are the pictures twain*
I promis'd you. Ah not (I hope) in vain
My efforts to arouse and entertain;
And if you ask me how I came to draw 'em,
This Governess and Guest, as if I saw 'em,
And think the portraits too high colour'd—well,
That Guest was I, and that cane-bearing belle
Was she who—but perhaps I'd best relate
The tale in proper form, at any rate.
So down to dinner did I take my way
To join the company, and tho' distrait
With all my mind still fixed on fustigation,
Manag'd to take part in the conversation;
And when it flagg'd, as talk is bound to do
In country houses all the country through,
I cunningly contriv'd to interject
That topic to which Mothers ne'er object:
"Your La'ship, and the children? Are they well?"
"Aye, Mr. Hardman, thank ye; but to tell
The truth, I'm far from being satisfied
With their Miss Lashley." Here she paus'd
and sighed.
"The pretty Governess, you mean?" I ask.
(My real int'rest I think best to mask)
"Well, plain or pretty, she must leave us soon—"
"How's that, my love?" his Lordship asks,
the spoon
Arrested half way from the serving platter:
"Miss Lashley leaving us? Why, what's
the matter?"

Amidst a *gen'ral laugh the subject dies;*
But it was plain who carried off the prize:
In this, as in all manner of retort,
My Lord was silenc'd; and I saw, in short
This governess so apt at flagellation
Was soon to be without a situation;
And as the meal and conversation sped,
A wondrous plan was hatching in my head.
Up rose the sun next day, and so did I
And hasten'd downstairs hoping to espy
The fair adept whose image all that night
Had filled my dreams with motions of delight
And, whether by some leading from Above
(Or elsewhere, if the pious disapprove),
I' th' garden, all alone, I found my love.
—I greet her with my most majestic bow;
She answers with a curtsey, fine and low:
I break the ice by mentioning the weather
And in no time we're walking on together.
O blessed hour when first I knew my Dear!
The image of that morning, cool and clear
Is at this moment present to my sight;
I see once more, with all the old delight,
The dewy garden in the light of dawn,
The pale sky and the little clouds thereon,
The slanting sunlight pouring in a flood,
Gilding the grass and silvering the wood;
And clearer still than all, I see once more
The dark blue capuchin my darling wore,
Within whose hood her face peep'd like a flower

Again I feel the dear disturbing charm
Of that first walk together, arm in arm
And once again, transpos'd in time, I hear
The low, sweet voice which then enthrall'd
my ear,
As we paced slowly o'er the dewy sod,
Discoursing on the Virtues of the Rod.

Tho' I already knew my "cruel fair"
Was no fond, visionary Doctrinaire
In matters of correction, soon I found
Her theory was, like her practice, sound,
Full of good reasons back'd by ancient saws
And moral apothegms and natural laws.
She preach'd most eloquently on the text
Of "proper measures"; and on this pretext
Seem'd to find full occasion to reveal
The fleshly taste behind the moral zeal;
But then, just when her accents made me feel
She look'd on whipping as an amorous bout,
She alter'd, and to plunge me into doubt,
Like Dante to his sinners parcelling out
She speaks of boys—"Look ye, Sir, they require
At different ages different instruments:
I give good measure in my punishments,
But would not task an infant with the weight
Of cutting whipcord: 'tis beyond his state.
No, no, indeed: although I do not shun
The strictest methods, when all's said and done
The naked palm is best for baby's skin;
Not till the boy is four should we begin
To use the leathern strap; and for the cane,
He must be eight ere he can stand the pain."
Tho' charm'd, I cast down a dissembling eye,
"Aye, aye, you're in the right", I make reply,
"But, Ma'am, you spoke of whipcord:
tell me, pray,
What is the age when that should come in play?"

She smil'd at that. O what a heavenly smile,
How well combin'd its gaiety and guile!
And in her eyes what sparkles of delight
Strove with the glow of wanton appetite!
Yet when she spoke, most circumspect and quiet
Her tone, as if the theme were dress or diet
Or other humdrum matter of debate:
"Why, Sir, the circumstances will dictate
The wisest course of action. Much depends
On the degree to which the boy offends;
His growth, his health and habits, too, control
The choice of instruments; but on the whole
'Tis my opinion, and has always been,
A boy should have the horsewhip at thirteen."
And thus we talk'd. Ah, how my Heart
did swell!
Her discourse charm'd me more than I can tell.

And still I took occasion oft to view
Her animated face, approv'd the hue
Of her complexion, brown but clear and warm,
Nor fail'd to note the beauties of her Form:
The length of limb, the slenderness of Waist
The amplitude of thigh—naught went untrac'd
By each inquiring and enraptur'd glance
I turn'd upon this queen of flagellants.
And, Reader, 'twas not long before I knew
My destiny—and what I had to do;
And tho' at first I found me rather queasy,
Once I had spoken, all the rest was easy.
My fortune and estate I did present,
So much in Consols and so much in rent;
My way of living, quiet and retir'd,
And how a wife was all that I desir'd,
No fond conceited girl whose feather head
Runs upon fashions and such ginger-bread,
No pert, well-dowered, London-loving Miss,
With dreams of naught save the metropolis,
Of Op'ra boxes, balls and carriages;
But some mature and sober votaress
Of home-grown pleasures in a homely dress—"
And here, observing how the brown and red
Bent in her cheek, "Some woman grown", I said,
"Some woman clear of head and firm of hand,
Whose natural disposition to command
Should find its scope and exercise within
Domestic rule and family discipline."
At these last words (insidiously stress'd)
I mark'd the sudden swelling of her breast,
The half-surpris'd unveiling of a glance
That met my own, like lance encountering lance;
And so I leapt into my peroration:
"In short, Miss Lashley, all my admiration
Is, as I find, directed to those spheres
Wherein the educative bent appears;
There have I sought my Bride, my happiness,
Have ask'd, 'Who better than a Governess?'"

A Short Biography of

EDITH CADIVEC

THE AUSTRIAN ALICE KERR-SUTHERLAND

Research by CANDIDA

THE YEAR 1924 WAS an unhappy one for lady disciplinarians of the old school. As all readers of this journal will know, Miss Alice Kerr-Sutherland spent that year inside Holloway Prison for Women, in North London, serving part of a sentence of four years which she had received for a series of public-morality convictions related to disciplinary activities—and in October of that same year, all known copies of her masterwork, *A Guide to the Correction of Young Gentlemen*, were seized in a police raid (and subsequently burned by court order). But the year had begun in even worse fashion for another lady of similar inclinations and skills, the 43-year-old Austrian schoolmistress Edith

Cadivec. On 3rd January, around five in the afternoon

> *My front doorbell rang loudly. I opened and to my great surprise four big burly men in civilian clothes pushed into my ante-chamber… they identified themselves as policemen…*

At this moment began a nightmare for Frau Cadivec and her daughter (also named Edith). Arrested, their house searched and various items and photographs confiscated, they were taken to the Morals Bureau where the younger Edith was instantly removed from her mother—they were not to meet again for some years. Frau Cadivec herself was duly brought to trial on a variety of charges relating to the flagellation of minors "and other lewd acts", and was sentenced to six years' penal servitude. Having served many months in solitary confinement, she attempted suicide (twice), and was released in December, 1925.

What had she done to deserve such treatment?

The facts are these, undisputed by either side. Frau Cadivec was a fanatical administratrix of physical discipline, her preferred culprits being adolescent girls, adolescent boys and adult males, in that order, and her preferred instrument being the birch-rod. She had long pursued a career as a girls' schoolmistress, but a year or two before, after a confused and peripatetic life—she had been married, though not happily—she and Edith returned to Vienna where she had set up a school for wayward children. Here she had boys under her charge for the first time.

> *Another youngster, the son of my ironing-woman, eleven-year-old Willy—whom I had known since he was born—came to me for extra help with his schoolwork. At his mother's request I checked his learning progress, and gave him writing and arithmetic assignments for the whole week so that he would not fail in school. He had to appear in my house every week, on Saturday. Willy was lazy and a ne'er-do-well who caused his worked-out mother a great deal of anguish. Therefore she pressed me to be very strict with the mendacious, wicked youngster and to thrash him soundly when he refused to obey. Willy personally brought me his mother's letters of complaint, in which she listed the mischief and the wanton pranks he had committed, and each time she urged me to mete out the punishment befitting him. According to the mother her youngster had great respect for me and my punishment, therefore, always had the best and most enduring effect…*
>
> *At the end of the tea-break, I tested the children and scrutinised their schoolwork. With Willy the written complaints of his mother sufficed to make him feel all my sternness. Moreover, he had learned nothing and had poorly prepared his schoolwork. He had to ask for his punishment, drop his trousers or put on punishment shorts, and he received his punishment either with the birch rod on the fully bared bottom or with the cane over the tightly fitting, tautly stretched punishment shorts. After the punishment he thanked me for it and kissed my hand.*

Soon afterwards she was arrested. The essence of the charges laid against were not so much that she had whipped her pupils on their bare bottoms with birch and cane—she did not deny it and indeed such punishments, not being at all rare in Germany and Austria in that period, did not constitute a *prima facie* offence—but that she had done in a lewd manner, to wit, before adult witnesses, and frequently at their request, with money changing hands. In other words, that she had operated a child-flagellation service for voyeurs. Few reading these words would object to her conviction for this, if it were true—the proper discipline of children is one thing; the gratification of voyeurs is another—

and indeed the court condemned her. In fact she resolutely denied any such activities, but was not believed.

The case was a sensation—just as it would be today. When Frau Cadivec emerged from prison, she found herself famous, after a fashion. Many people had written to her in prison, in any case, and she was invited to appear on lecture tours, where she spoke vigorously in defence of corporal punishment for children, lovingly administered by mothers and schoolmistresses. She was revealed to have developed an almost mystical sense of the rightness of her actions. and she set a good deal of this down in her first book, *Confessions and Experiences*, published in 1930 for a limited readership of scientists, sociologists and medical men.

Frau Cadivec had admirers in many countries where her case had been publicised, but none were more passionate than the young Danish schoolmistress Senta von Lohstein. In the case of Frau Cadivec an erotic motivation for the administration of corporal punishment is acknowledged—it forms a cornerstone of her child-rearing theories—but it is not the only motive: the well-being of the child is also extolled. No such graces complicated Miss Von Lohstein's system: also entrusted with the power to apply the birch to errant girls, she did so with only one aim in mind—her own gratification, luridly described again and again—and as a result hers is a far less attractive personality.

We know of the correspondence between these two women, which eventually grew into a physical relationship, because it forms the greater part of Frau Cadivec's second book *Eros: the Meaning of my Life*, published in about 1931. Both books were, of course, written in German, and languished unread (except by doctors, sociologists &c) for many years until in 1971 they were translated for the New York publisher Grove Press. Grove produced hardback and paperback editions, but both books have been out of print for at least fifteen years and are becoming hard to find. They remain the only known English translations.

A summary of Edith Cadivec's life shews that she may have had little choice in the matter of her disciplinary persona. As a child she had been rigorously disciplined in a shaming manner, with the inevitable birch—wielded by one of those stepmothers who make the grisliest stepmother stories seem terrifyingly plausible—and there had never been any doubt in her mind what she wanted to do when she grew up. She wished to pass on the birch discipline she had received, and to that end immediately began a career as a schoolmistress, in a small Paris convent school. There the rod was in frequent, and luscious use:

> *A red coir carpet lay across the length and breadth of the yellow flagstone floor. The single Gothic window, with coloured panes, formed a deep niche in the wall. The light filtered into the room through the red-blue-green-yellow-violet chequered window panes and endowed the objects with a magic effect. Even the faces of the persons entering the room were changed by the iridescent reflected light, flickering restlessly and lighting up in all hues. Near the window, freely accessible from all sides, stood an armless and backless sofa-like bench, stiffly upholstered and covered with brown leather. A leather strap with a buckle was attached in the middle of each side of this item of furniture. To the left of the window, in the corner, stood a more than life-size crucifix with the tortured figure of the Crucified that dominated the room and gave it an uncanny note. A broad, low cupboard with a drawer and two doors stood to the right of the window against the wall. In the background of the room was a long prayer-stool to the right and left of which were two old-fashioned high-backed leather armchairs with hollowed-out seats which looked as though the sitters had fallen asleep and died in them…*

> *As we entered here, Marie-Therese* [one of the disciplinary nuns] *betook herself to the cupboard, opened the closed doors and let me peer inside. Arranged according to size, I saw the different kinds of instruments of punishment hanging from hooks: leather straps and lashes in all lengths and magnitudes, cat-o'-nine tails, leather martinets with long, broad, or edged belts, short martinets made of twisted hemp cords with large knots for castigations, birches for scourging the whole body, thin and flexible canes covered with fine leather, while in the right corner of the chest's interior a number of fresh birches, placed in a clay pitcher filled to the brim with salt water, sprouted, so to speak, up to the lifeless punishment instruments. I learned that all these instruments served the nuns for the penances and castigations which the strict Order prescribed for the mortification of the flesh of its adepts. None of us spoke a word.*
>
> *Amazed and deeply stirred by the unusual profusion of these secret things, I stared into the chest while Marie-Therese expertly selected from the pitcher a fresh birch rod soaked for softening. She let it hiss through the air several times in order to shake the moisture off its thin twigs. The sibilance of the birch aroused my nerves. I feel that no other punishment instrument can be compared with the birch. The birch, the birch, always the birch! It is the sweetest and most shaming way for meting out punishment to big fourteen-year-old girls. Moreover, Marie-Therese, according to her instructions, uses only the birch. The cane is used only over the drawers, which is not in keeping with her taste. It must be the naked bottom…*

Readers of Miss Kerr-Sutherland's book will already have noted the close resemblance between her punishment room—with its stained-glass window, so proudly described, and its atmosphere of religious atonement—and the punishment room described above. Indeed the two women, and their respective careers, seem to have followed oddly coördinated patterns, so much so that if both women are not separately known to have existed, one might suppose the one to be both fictional and "based upon" the other! Both were avid disciplinarians who saw themselves as Eternal Mothers; both favoured the birch above all other instruments; and both flourished—and were cast down—in the period immediately after the Great War. It will not be thought a coincidence that both had experienced severe upbringings in which the rod was a feature of daily use. It would indeed be tantalising to speculate whether or not they ever corresponded, but no evidence for this exists.

The great difference between them seems to be that while Miss Kerr-Sutherland preferred to discipline males, Frau Cadivec concentrated upon her own sex. Though not a Lesbian, she was a mystical feminist of an early and almost forgotten type (though she has her spiritual descendants around the world to this very day), and above all a mystical maternalist. Her justification for the hundreds of birchings, canings and spankings she administered throughout her "working life" (and afterwards, in a private capacity) was that of the Disciplinary Mother. She acknowledged a strong erotic impulse, but claimed it should not be separated out from the greater Self—why, she asks again and again in her writings, should a highly necessary activity be frowned upon or outlawed simply because Eros also makes his presence known? (Many mothers will freely and honestly acknowledge an erotic stimulus in the act of breast-feeding; but nobody this century has claimed that for this reason alone the practice should be regarded as a form of child abuse. The good of the child is pre-eminent; the erotic impulse is secondary, cannot be avoided, and irrelevant.)

> *How often I got into the situation of having to take over children who were the products of a misguided pedagogy and then of having to take effect on them*

in the right way! How often parents begged me not to tolerate negligence and disobedience from their offspring! Such pleas appealing to the authority of the teacher were an expression of the parents' own weakness in child-rearing. It made me happy to transform lazy, recalcitrant young people into tractable pupils, eager to learn, to convert indolence into industriousness and disobedience into obedience; this, naturally, was attainable only through strict discipline.

I understood that young people unconditionally need and recognise the unrestricted guidance of a very strict mother or teacher if they are to grow up into really worthwhile human beings. Out of deepest conviction I most thoroughly applied rod and cane as the final embodiment of pedagogical authority and always achieved the best educational results with this.

I always acted only in agreement with the parents whenever I had to inflict disciplinary punishment that actually belonged in the province of the home. The young people also wanted—and had to be—handled sternly and they gladly oriented themselves according to the will of a person held in respect, in whose salutary discipline they felt sheltered and good at the same time.

I maintained strict order during instruction. Although the pupils never heard me utter a word of anger, they had a boundless respect for me. For those concerned, I had an incredibly painful and shaming way of reprimand when, in icy calm, I left the poorly prepared student to his stuttering embarrassment and, after a breathchoking pause, pronounced judgment with a stern, curt "so and so many."

This was the sharpest expression of my censure and it signified the number of birch blows that would be owing to his or her naked bottom for laziness. No matter how hard the lessons were which I prepared for my male and female pupils, they experienced them as a recognition that I credited their intelligence so much that I made high demands on them…

One does not teach by a method or a system, but rather by personality. The stream of spontaneous naturalness, goodness, and sternness in thoughts, feelings, and actions that flows from a maternally receptive woman to her surroundings is infinitely more marvellous in its effect than all pedagogic theories.

Unfortunately there can be little doubt that these fine feelings and heroic philosophies were not always observed by Frau Cadivec with the meticulous propriety one might expect. She may not have intended to confuse the disciplinary and the erotic—and in her own mind there may have been no difficulty distinguishing between the two—but there can be little doubt that she gave any number of hostages to fortune. The best one can say is that she was astonishingly naïve, for to apply a physical punishment to an adolescent girl in the presence of male visitors is, by all standards, highly improper. She did this time and again, and so made it easy for the authorities to convict her.

At the same time the case has ugly resonances with scandals in this country during the latter part of the twentieth century, particularly Cleveland, Rochdale and Orkney. Children formerly in her charge—including her own daughter—were bullied into making statements which are emphatically declared (with a ring of real conviction) to be false. She was said to have sexually abused her daughter, for example. Young Edith signed a statement alleging as much, but it later turned out that she had been threatened with years in an institution if she did not. She afterwards withdrew the allegations and mother and daughter were re-united.

Later on in her astonishing career she attracted a number of would be male lovers—many wrote to her, one or two on a regular basis. In a letter to the most devoted of these followers she speaks for all dominant women of taste and sensibility when she chides him for his "false submissiveness".

It was not because you exposed your innermost fantasies to me that I became angry with you but because you intoxicated yourself with your selfish voluptuary pleasure and pandered to your canine rut.... in your letter you speak in a tone which does not befit you. You indulge in too much phrasemaking, relate too much trivia, and have the arrogance to have your own opinion. That is not your right, it does not befit you! And still another thing irritates me, makes me angry with you—the impropriety of your "commands." Thus you anticipate the most ecstatic events, rob them of their spontaneity and of all attraction!

I will also no longer hear of your speaking of yourself as "slave"! I despise this word as insipid and farcical; I have always found it hateful. It is a stupid, foolish, meaningless word, a hackneyed, ugly expression which, moreover, has an evil aftertaste...

You are not my "slave," you are my loyally devoted, self-sacrificing maidservant who is a part of me and whose feminine-child soul has merely gone astray in external male form. Your daily prayer should read: "Behold, I am the maidservant of my mistress and the maleness in me is most deeply detested!"

It is not known what happened to her. As citizens of Austria, she and her daughter would have become part of the German Reich after the 1938 Anschluss. At that time Frau Cadivec would have been 58 or 59—eerily, almost exactly the same age as Miss Kerr-Sutherland. But if she or her daughter survived the Second World War, no-one can say. Like her great Scots contemporary, the rest of her life is shrouded in mystery.

'THE GOVERNESS' GALLERY

The depiction of Nursery Rhymes in children's books was once less "correct" (and more honest) than it is today; as these early 19th century vignettes show.

Jack and Jill went up the hill
to fetch a pail of water

Jack fell down and broke his crown
And Jill came tumbling after

When Jill came in, how she did grin
To see Jack's paper plaster
Her mother, vexed, did whip her next
For laughing at Jack's disaster

Tom, Tom the piper's son
Stole a pig and away did run
The pig was eat, and Tom was beat
And Tom went howling down the street

Little Polly Flinders sat among the cinders
Warming her pretty little toes
Her mother came and caught her
and whipped her little daughter
For spoiling her nice new clothes.

The Amiable Genius of LOUIS MALTESTE

The early 20th century produced an extraordinary explosion in erotic art and literature, almost all of the best work emanating from Paris. As if to give the lie to the ancient French fiction that Disciplinism is "un vice anglaise", a great deal of this work relates to the use of the Rod—albeit, in a particularly (and to many, delightful) French mode.

*The creations of **Louis Malteste**, alias the author **Jacques D'Icy**, tower above the other work of this period. Malteste—whose real name is not known—was that rare type of artist: the bi-talented. Not only did he write the most delicious novels of the period, but he also illustrated them. Working mainly in charcoal and pencil, he created—ostensibly as book illustrations—a series of over 100 exquisite scenes of Discipline which remain, in the opinion of many cognoscenti, among the best ever produced.*

Aside from the obvious excellence of his technique, the keynotes of Malteste's drawings are, firstly, abundant good humour — there is often a burlesque note which gives an unmistakably French air—and secondly, his clear preference for scenes where females punish other females (though the punishment of boys by young women was another favourite topic).

*Malteste published a series of novels between 1912 and 1930. His first was **Qui Aime Bien** (Châtie Bien); this was followed by **Monsieur Paulette** and **Paulette Trahie** (Paulette Betrayed, sometimes called Paulette's Film, the only one ever to be translated into English, by Janus Books 1974), and afterwards by **Les Mains Chèries**, **Suzanne Écuyère** and **Fifi L'Arpête**.*

Many of these were originally published by Orties Blanches of Paris: some have been reprinted by Editions Dominic Leroy of that same city, though all titles are currently in French.

Monsieur Paulette
et ses Épouses

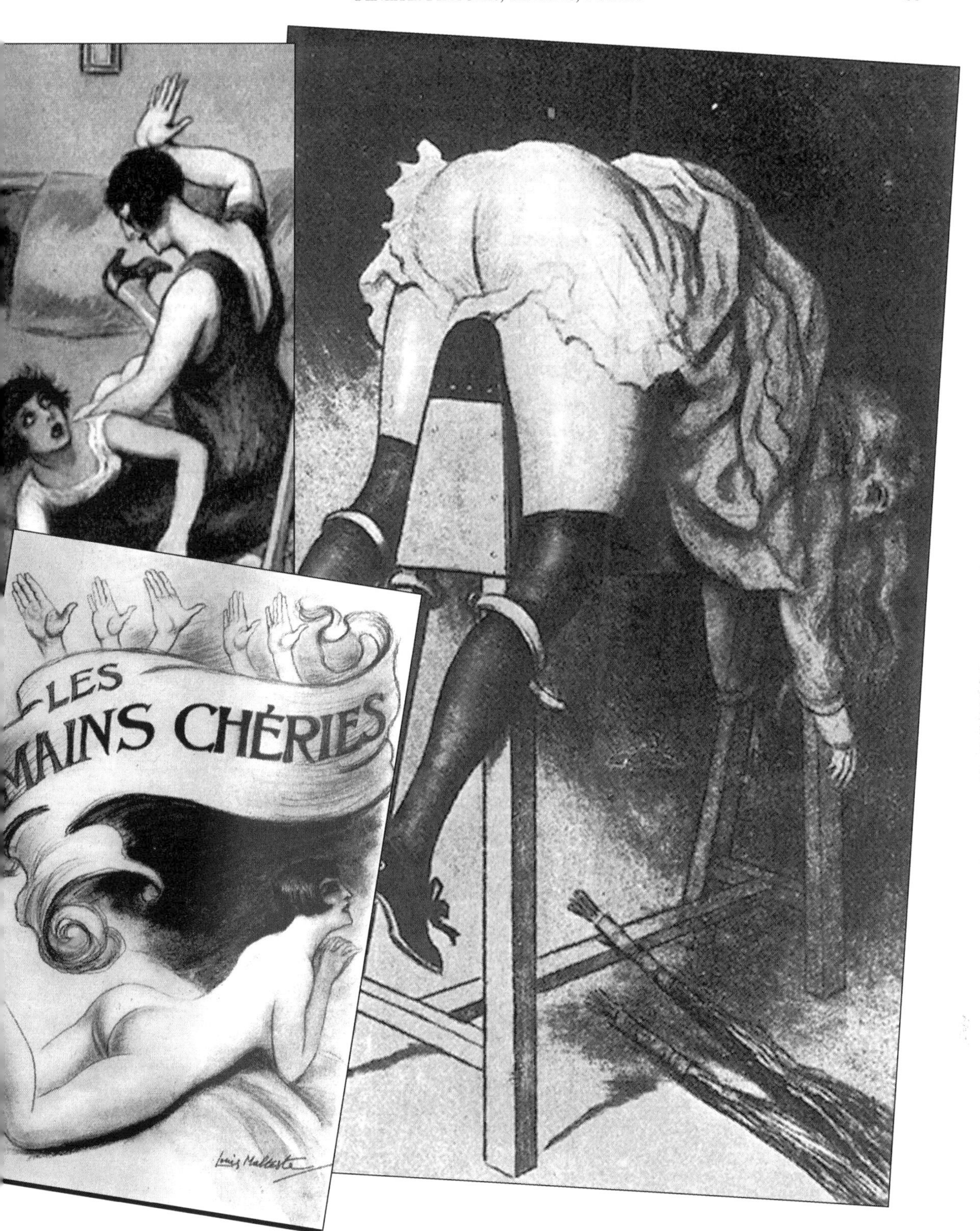
LES
MAINS CHÉRIES

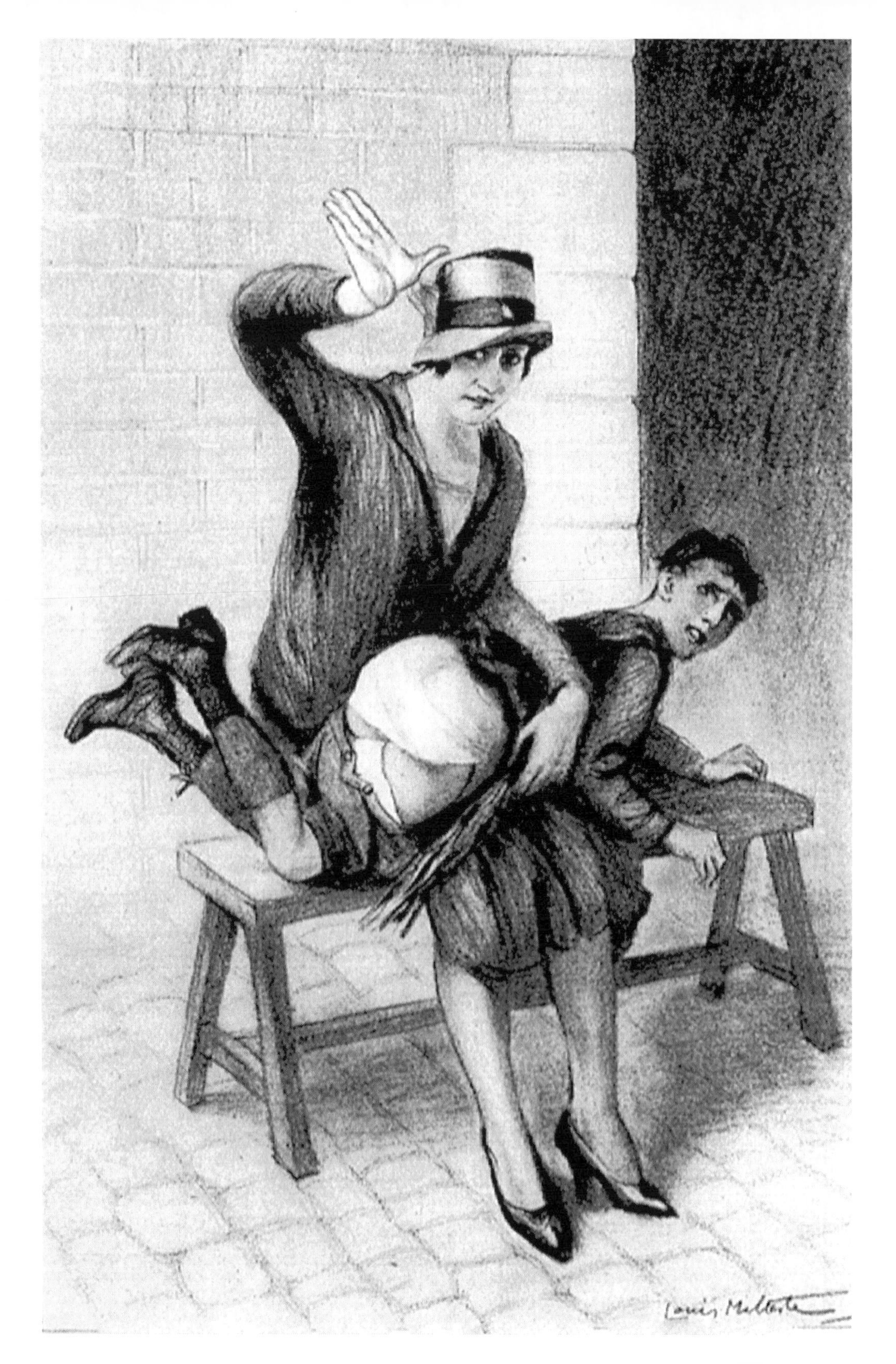

PUNISHMENT DAY

It's Punishment Day at the Orphanage,
It's Punishment Day today!
A score or more of the juvenile poor
Have been "booked" for breaking
Orphanage law,
Each tick of the clock, as the hands creep round
Brings nearer the hour when trousers come down
When frocks will be raised, and petticoats too
(It's rumoured her Ladyship's coming to view)
Twenty-three doomed little waifs and strays
Enduring the shame of a Punishment Day,

Apart from the flock, they shuffle and weep
(It's certain not one of them's had any sleep)
Sternly watched by a bonneted nurse
They wonder if Life can hold anything worse
Than the Fate each one of them knows lies in store
The price of exceeding Orphanage law!
The oldest are silent, the little ones cry,
"There'll be more tears to come", thinks the nurse,
"By-and-by!"
Now each of the Doomed hears the chink of the gate.
As usual, her Ladyship's ten minutes late!

"Some sherry, your Ladyship?"—"Thank you,
I will.
Pray tell me, how many are on today's bill?"
"Three-and-twenty, m'lady. E'en now they await".
"Then let us not stand between them and their fate;
Which is richly deserved, I presume? As I thought.
These urchins, I fear, can only be taught
By means of the rod; though it's for their own good."
"M'lady, your precepts are well understood,
Rest assured; while I remain Matron-in-chief,
No whining or cringing or feigning of grief,
Will come between me and my duty!"—"It's clear,
That you and your staff hold these brats'
welfare dear.
They're lucky—why, thank you! Perhaps one
more glass
I was saying: normally, brats of their class,
Live and die on the street, among litter and worse.
Never knowing the joys —"
"Yes, what is it, Nurse?"
"Matron, Milady, Assembly's complete".
"More sherry?"—"No thank you; I vow I'm replete.
I'd prefer to proceed"—"Then shall we go down?"
"By all means." In due course the ominous sound,
Of footfalls on stairs can be heard down below
Where "patrons" await the start of the "show".

The Guest is enthron'd, the Matron presides,
While gathered away in a group to one side,
Are the twenty-three criminals, ashen of face
Averting their eyes from the scene on the dais,
Where two under-matrons, brawny of thew,
Are arranging the ferrules in sequence of use.
For males under ten (and females, of course)
It's the strap; of the Scottish kind known
as a "tawse".
Four of these are laid out in order of harm,
While a bundle of canes, as thick as your arm
Is unwrapped, and the rattans arranged in like wise,
For easy selection. Already the eyes
Of those culprits whose ages are 'twixt twelve
and ten,
Are awash with the dread expectation of pain.
This collection of culprits is full-well aware
That the canes are intended for use on their rears!

For such is the System: those brats under eight,
Who transgress, are smacked on the uncovered nates
There and then, on the spot, by a summary nurse.
Over eight, and your fate is immediately worse.
The strap is for you; and in full public view
Past ten, and you sample a different brew,
To wit, you'll be caned in a most shameful way,
And, just like the others, on Punishment Day!
But those culprits whose hearts give the
mightiest lurch
Are those over twelve, awaiting—the Birch!
Already a basket of rods has appeared,
Each bound up with ribbon, a bouquet of Fear
Of differing lengths, and of differing kind
And each purpose-built for one naughty behind.
And made, what is more, as tradition demands,
By th' intended victims, whose trembling hands,
Have assembled the rods more than three days ago.
O visions of terror ! O symbols of woe !

A dread silence falls; from the Matron—a look,
And a pinafore'd urchin brings forward the Book
It's placed on the lectern; and now Matron stands
Advances; and leafs through the Book with her hand.
The twenty-three quiver; the watchers await;
Her Ladyship smiles; 'tis the instant of Fate.
"John Cobham!" says Matron—a small
culprit quails;
"For failing, as ordered, to slop out the pails
Tuesday last—an even four strokes with the tawse!
Isaac Kettle! Infringing the 'No Talking' laws,
In like fashion earns four. Now come out!"
White of face,
The pair shuffle out. As they draw near the dais,
Two maids come to meet them; a maid for each boy.
With hands out in greeting, a gesture of joy,
As it seems for an instant; then small hands
are grasped
Each nurse spins around without loosing her clasp
And both boys are hoisted on broad female backs
The two under-matrons, with movements relaxed,
Unfasten the buttons at front, back and side
The two pairs of trousers, unfasten'd, now slide
From their normal position—that's to say, on
the hips,
—To a place lower down, under Gravity's grip…

The first "horse" stoops forward: the target's
raised fair
A bullseye, a sight-mark, a peach in mid-air.
A strap-wielding matron, determined of face
Takes a sharpshooter's aim at the obvious place
A swing of her wrist, a flicker, a smack!
John Cobham leaps high on the maidservant's back
From six feet away comes a whack! and a bleat
Where a similar tickle's applied to the seat

Of young Isaac Kettle, whose ungovern'd speech
Is likewise paid off with a bare, smarting breech.
One after the other the strokes are applied
The air of the hall rings with penitent cries
Till each has had four, the punition ordained
And is promising never to transgress again.
With hands joined on head, and breeches still low
With shirt-tails still rumpled, and bottoms aglow,
They're marched to one side and stood to the wall
In view of everyone there in the hall
The strappers and holders enjoy a brief pause
While more names are spoken, those doomed to the tawse
James Callow, Jack Rother, Rob Tucker, Will Dare,
Are called to the front and then hoisted in pairs.
Two by two, rumps are bared and the leather laid home
Soon eleven sniffling urchins stand, face to the stone.
The strap's turn is done; the Matron again
Reads out names from the Book, of those doomed to the cane.

A different procedure now comes into force
For the style of the cane is distinct from the tawse
A culprit's expected to march bravely forward
Bending over a chair to receive his award
First having—perforce—to uncover his rear
Exposing pale skin to the cane's bitter sear.
The first boy advances, shuffling of gait
A plea on his lips… 'till he sees it's too late.
With a gulp and a fumble, the trousers fall down
He bends over the chair with a whimpering sound.
The first under-matron now chooses a switch
From the several canes laid out on the table-top. Which
Of these many ferrules will be meet for his hide?
It's a consequence only fesseuses can decide.
She gauges his backside, assesses his strength
And chooses a cane of considerable length.
Five strokes the award; the cane's in mid-air
She uncoils her wrist and it lands full and square.
A snap! and a yelp! and a voice intones "One!"
There'll be more snaps—and yelps—'ere this caning is done.
On four more occasions the cane hums and whines
Crackling across his presented behind.
On four more occasions a voice counts the score
While each time his bottom's grown steadily rawer.

Yet he's acted with courage; the five searing skelps
He's endured with nothing more anguished than yelps
There's been no bid for freedom, no dash for the door
(In any case all know what then lies in store
The chastisement proper, severely laid on
—And then yet another, for trying to run.
That's double the punishment; better by far
To suffer five strokes across your derrière.)
His courage rewarded with gesture of grace,
The stripling is spared the usual disgrace
He pulls up his trousers and hastens away
The first of those caned on this Punishment Day!
But by no means the last: nine more candidates hover
Each ready, in turn, to untruss and bend over.
Of the nine, eight are boys, as is normally found
Wherever such wilful delinquents abound;
The tenth to be caned is young Emma O'Toole
Quite simply the naughtiest girl in the school.
At twelve years of age, she's been spanked hard, of course;
She's been o'er Matron's lap and been whipped with a tawse
But as she's continued to sin, it's ordained
That Emma O'Toole shall be publicly caned.

Her name is pronounced; and Emma is there;
With smock hoisted high she bends over the chair.
Her drawers tumble down; her bottom is ready;
The hands that hold fast are perfectly steady
Her jaw is clenched tight; she's determined to try
And prove to the lads that big lasses don't cry.
The first of the three strokes she's destined to bear
Arrives with a wallop—and now, sudden fear
That she won't last the distance; a second stroke lands
With a shriek she stands up; and her ungovern'd hands
Fly to pamper the spot so outraged by the cane;
And though she immediately bends o'er again
The damage is done. For avoiding her licks
The number of cuts is exalted to six.
No chances are taken; she's held on her face
While the four strokes are laid on the Biblical place.
She's placed to the wall and stands, smock hoisted high
And now we perceive that big lasses do *cry.*

The chair and the canes are hustled from sight
Replaced in the centre by visions of fright:
The symphony's climax is now fully due

And the basket of birches is placed in clear view.
"How many," Milady now asks, "did you say
Are due to be birched on this Punishment Day?"
"Two culprits, your Ladyship", Matron replies
"For dreadful debauchery, and telling of lies."
"Debauchery, Matron?"—"Milady, 'tis so.
The vile thing occurred not more than two days ago.
When the villains were found, there was naught they could say.
And I vowed they'd be flogged on this Punishment Day!"
"They were found do you say? What condition was this?"
"Milady, I hesitate"—"Yet I insist."
"I'll tell you, Milady, with sadness and grief
For it shows how the Evil One works his mischief.
These two, Edwin Murray and Mortimer Stead
Consorted together; they shared the same bed!"
"And what style of punishment have you decreed,
A fitting riposte to this depravé deed?"
"Milady, to chastise these villainous hides,
Two dozen, I thought, that's a dozen each side."
"And what are their ages?"—"Both have fourteen years."
"Then twenty-four lashes is too much to bear." —"Milady?"
—"Dear Matron, our cause in this place,
Is to salvage the débris of our human race
And by all means—that includes Justice's Sword—
To bring to our charges the Love of the Lord.
The Rod is our ally, our servant, our friend
But not, of itself, the only sure end.
To punish too violently is a mistake
The souls in our keeping are not ours to break.
A surfeit of cruelty evokes the wrong mood
And two dozen birch-strokes will surely draw blood."

THE MATRON dissembles; in fact, she's astounded
To hear views such as these from Milady propounded.
She's amazed (it wouldn't be too much to say)
To hear such opinions on Punishment Day!
Yet she errs in her judgment: Milady's not mild;
Neither sparing the rod, nor spoiling the child
"This crime is so shameful, that Shaming must play
A particular part in this Punishment Day!
A notion I have: it's to take these two flirts
And forcibly dress them in maidchildren's skirts.
With pinafores, bonnets and black stockings too
It ought to provide the most interesting view!
When birching a boy, the mode I prefer
Is the untrusséd youth bending over a chair
Or a stool or a table or any low thing
To accept, on his own, the chastisement's sting.
By displaying the courage a boy should possess
He salvages dignity under duress.
But from girls we expect less heroics, I fear
Less courageous than boys, girls are more prone to tears
They wriggle, and shuffle, and cover, and fend
And try to evade the ferrule that descends.
For this reason they're horsed: it prevents further fuss
An ideal posture for being untrussed.
If we treat your two culprits like wise, I should say
Then they'll always remember this Punishment Day!
To be whipp'd like two girls for their degraded deed?
A dozen sharp strokes will be all that we need!"

THE MATRON'S convinced; she summons a nurse
And raps out commands in sentences terse.
The nurse drops a curtsey and hastens away
There follows a lull in this Punishment Day!
A minute—five minutes—of silence are shared
Then enters a nurse: "Madam, all is prepared!"
Her Ladyship nods, and so Matron does too
A doleful procession then comes into view
Two great girls, it seems, are led to the dais
Their smocks and their pinafores neatly in place
Their bonnets are fastened, their girdles are clasped
Each carries a birch-spray in trembling grasp.
And, kneeling to offer the soon-to-be-used rods,
Each "maid" humbly begs to be properly flogged.
Like girls they are horsed; and their smocks are pulled high
Exposing white bloomer as far as mid-thigh
These pants are unfasten'd and eased off the hips
Each bottom prepared for the punitive whip.
Milady advances; she flexes her wrist
She chooses the rod with the wickedest kiss.
The Matron does likewise; both whipping dames stand
At the operative angle, with birch-rods in hand…

AND AS the rods hover, dear reader, I pray
Let us take tactful leave of this Punishment Day!

A tantalising finish from the anonymous original author, but that wasn't the end of the story. In Issue 4 we published a "sequel", written by the artist CURTUS, which provided a delightful "coda"…

THE EAGER assembly leans forward with glee,
The better these pinafore'd boobies to see.
In the breathless hush, not a sound can be heard
But the whimper of culprits (who look quite absurd).
Then Milady and Matron exchange a brief look
And the Rod comes to bring these rash lovers to book
With a swish!—an explosion!—two howls sound as one
And the terrible Punishment Dance has begun.
"Swish-switt!" sing the first one. The yells ring out loud.
"Swish-switt!" goes the next, to the awe of the crowd.
A bellow is torn from young Mortimer's lips
As he brazenly flaunts his fast-reddening hips
Whilst Edwin is blubbing in desperate shame
His bare bottom writhing (it feels bathed in flame!)
All masculine pride is quite driven away
From these boys-in-girls'-dresses on Punishment Day!
The juniors, long lacking a reason to smile
Are nudging and winking with mirth all the while.
To witness big seniors punished like this
Is a sight that each brat would not willingly miss!
And pretty young lasses of seven or eight
Take delight in the sight of the miscreants' fate!
For they know this disgrace of young Edwin and Morty
Is a fitting reward for their both being naughty!

AT LAST, after six strokes, the mid-point is reached
Through tears, some remission is humbly beseeched
But the pitiful words merely bring forth disdain
With a change of fresh "horses", the woe starts again.
Now Mortimer's rump is Milady's to thrash
While Matron poor Edwin commences to lash.
What a screech now is torn from the throat of young Stead
And Murray is sure he'd be better off dead.
Now horsed by fresh maids, they still struggle with fright—
They really both make a contemptible sight.
Edwin's bonnet is off; he's in such disarray.
While Mortimer's drawers have been quite kicked away.
Their bottoms are crimson, so swollen and sore,
And covered with weals that are angry and raw.
For these two howling "lasses", their eyes filled with tears
This unusual birching's confirmed their worst fears
Each child who is watching knows how, from here on,
These ninnies will pay, now their status is gone.
For all the young orphans are sure to enjoy
The teasing (and worse!) of each well-disgraced boy.
"Oh, stop! Please have mercy! Have mercy, we pray!"
Squeal the boys-in-girls'-frocks on this Punishment Day.
And the orphans all giggle to see such big boys weep
As they shriek in high voices, so normally deep
Such begging, such pleading, such feminine tears
The mixture is music to juvenile ears!

THE PUNISHMENT ends; and the rods are thrown down
Milady examines each boy with a frown.
Her words are most scathing: "Despicable creatures,
You've quite lost the right to resume your male breeches.
In skirts you'll remain, for a full thirty days.
Perhaps this will teach you to mend your bad ways!"
"Oh no, not wear frocks!" The two quake with fear
While the audience, in rapture, gives vent to a cheer!
"But that's not the end of your shame, my young beauties.
I'll have you instructed in kitchen-maid's duties,
With this one refinement, to add to your woe,
Those skirts will be pinned up, your bottoms to show.
No drawers will protect you from communal gaze,
And in that condition you'll serve thirty days.
And as the red fades, as most sadly it must,
We'll paint it anew, as a cure for your lust!"

THE CULPRITS depart, their bottoms displayed.
Those naughty young "maids" at their fate are dismayed
To scrub and to dust, and to polish, and peel
With the laughter of all following on at their heel.
Milady departs, to return to the Hall
Her day, although long, has been pleasantly full
With mood thus elated (it must now be said)
This night, what delight will Milord have in bed!
So as the sun sets, dear Reader, I pray
Look back, and remember this Punishment Day.
For if you're not good and honest and true,
This fearful chastisement might happen to you! ✤

Tables Turned, by the American sculptress Erin, celebrates the rediscovery by Modern Woman of her ancient disciplinary powers.

Its creation took nine months, using the "Lost Wax" casting method of bronze founding. It is a composite sculpture of two couples, each in their own disciplinary embrace, 18 inches high, in solid cast bronze on a formica base.

Both pairs were created in a Limited Edition of 15 apiece and are sold separately at $3,900, or together in the full *Tables Turned* composite, at $7,500.

BOOK REVIEW:

A Queenly Offering

THE *Queen of the Grove* is a remarkable attempt to re-invoke the style and feel, both literary and artistic, of a bygone era of disciplinary erotica—the so-called "Golden Age" of the 1920s and 30s. Written by Miss Louise Malatesta *[the pen-name for a valued Member of this Society—Editors]*, illustrated by the artist Sardax and published by Chardmore Press (an imprint of Tim Woodward Publishing Ltd.)*, this is no single novel, nor a manual like the *Guide*, but a 170-page collection of short stories, poems and illustrations, the entire book attractively designed, printed and bound in dark green hardcovers with silver lettering. There is also a laminated jacket depicting a legendary figure—a "Green Woman", presumably the Queen (Goddess?) of the title. It's a collector's piece even before one opens it.

The illustrations are what first catch the eye. Were it not for the disciplinary theme that appears here and there (but never vulgarly or obtrusively), these excellent and lyrical pieces of line work could have been drawn for one of the better children's books of the period—when this form of art was at its height. Sardax has the highest of reputations in this field, of course, and to secure his services for this project has been a coup of the first magnitude. In addition to many exquisite full- and double-page plates, he has created dozens of pieces of lovely, jewel-like "page furniture"—corner embellishments, marginalia, dropped capitals and illuminated chapter titles [see these pages for examples]. There is excellent sympathy between artist and author, and if one didn't know both principals personally one might be tempted to say that, as in the case of "Louis Malteste"

*Original publisher. Now AKS Books Ltd

and "Jacques D'Icy" **[see page 82]** they are one and the same person.

Miss Malatesta's writing is also excellent. Her short stories reveal an impressive breadth of interests, and all are written with the authority that comes from true passion allied to self control and the strong desire to make the telling of a good story her first priority. There are seven, ranging from the delightfully optimistic "Eleanor's System" with its uproarious trick ending, to the unexpected and moving mercy which crowns the endeavours of "The Vigilantes of Durnley Parva", a group of boarding school girls determined to teach the village bully a lesson. There's a shock of another kind in store for readers of "Dameschool".

Black comedy gives way to epic tragedy in "The Three Gifts of the Dowager August Jade", the longest story in the collection and, perhaps because of the remoteness of 17th century China, where it is set, the least accessible: it operates on an heroic scale and delves deep into Chinese legend for the tale of the Dragon Whips of Szechuan and the fateful consequences of their use. This story is also the setting for some of Sardax's most spectacular illustrations.

There are poems, too. On the evidence of "That Gioconda Smile" alone, Miss Malatesta is no less accomplished in this field than in prose and tale-telling, but in most cases she prefers to use her talent to pastiche others, mainly (for some reason) Kipling, though here again she displays affection as well as expertise and humour.

Miss Hathaway stands
with the birch in her hand
and my heart plummets down past my knees.
The vision is Godlike;
she swishes the rod
like a westerly wind in the trees

Many readers will judge that Miss Malatesta's finest moments in this collection arrive with the two stories "No Option" and "The Queen of the Grove". Each tells, in its own way, of an unusual interaction (of a disciplinary nature) between a boy and an older female. In the former case, an English boys' prep school of the 1920s is the scene for an moving, intensely romantic variation on the standard "Harriet Marwood" plot. The second, more mystical, puts a kindly and learned paganism at the disposal of Justice; a dreamlike story which begins with a catastrophic moorland fire and ends on a sweet and expiatory note.

The Queen of the Grove is a credit to all concerned, not least to its publishers, who are to be congratulated for restoring to public view a form of literature which many had thought extinct. Let us hope there are more to follow.

CANDIDA

Belle-Mère

By Louise Malatesta

From *The Queen of the Grove*

O WHY DO YOU *stand there, pale youth with no name*
Hiding your face to the wall?
Your whole situation suggestive of shame
All by yourself in the hall.
Why is your attitude one of defeat?
Why are your trousers pulled down to your feet?
And what caused those vivid red stripes on your seat?
To whom are you so much in thrall?

Your belle-mère, *you say? Twenty minutes ago?*
And what was the cause of it, pray?
A failure to construe "that bore Cicero"?
My lad, better watch what you say.
I'm a friend of your belle-mère, *so be circumspect*
Be familiar with me and I'll tell her direct
I've strong reason to think you know what to expect!
Don't make a mistake in this way.

Return to your story: what rod did she wield?
What lash raised those furrows behind?
A cane? You surprise me. I'd guess that those weals
Meant a scourge of the many-tailed kind
A miniature "cat" like the French martinet
A fistful of osiers au vinaigrette
A flail of cords, knotted—but much better yet
Is a birch-rod of classic design.

And where did it happen, pale youth with wry face,
The correction you latterly got?
The bedroom's a very conventional place
Yet you say you were whipped on the spot?
Right here in the hall with the servants in view?
That certainly was a severe thing to do
Even to such a rapscallion as you
Or—then again—possibly not.

So how were you postured, O youth with red eyes?
Were you made to bend over a chair?
The traditional method when chaps of your size
Are thrashed clean of the sins that they bear
You were forced o'er a table, with maids holding fast?
Your breeches unbuttoned and pulled to half-mast?
Then you knew how it felt to be cornered at last
As you heard the cane swish in the air!

And how many strokes did your belle-mère *inflict*
While you lay on the table in fear?
An orthodox, generally merciful "six"?
Or was she especially severe?
A dozen's enough with a well-handled cane
Add six more, and few culprits come back again
While two dozen draws near to the summit of pain
When a rattan's applied to the rear.

Then afterwards—did she compel you to kneel
And thank her for clearing the score?
After kissing the rod, in a lachrymose squeal
Did you deem yourself sinless—but sore?
Expecting dismissal, you were bidden instead
To remain in the hall with your hands on your head
With bottom and face both the same shade of red…
…We're back where we came in, once more.

'THE GOVERNESS' GALLERY

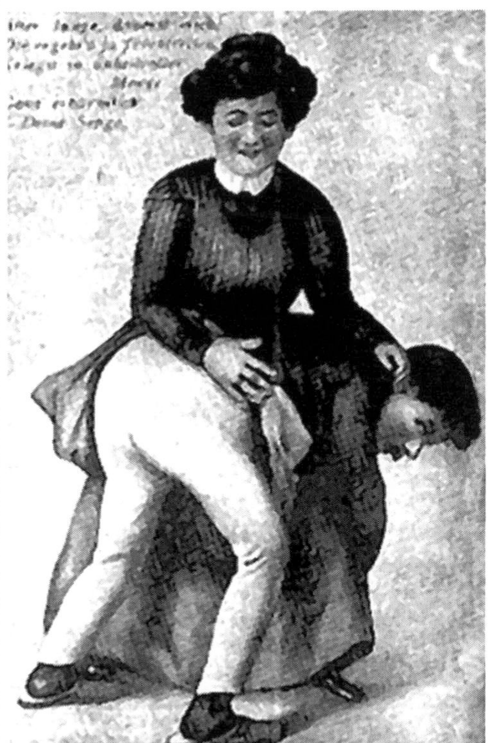

THE MATRIARCH chastises the whole family. As Venus, she punishes boy-Cupid (top left) in this 17th-century allegory. She appears again, birching an adolescent, on a mediæval church carving (lower right). In an 18th-century French painting upper right) she disciplines *en famille*, while in the late 19th-century postcard, from Germany (lower left), she executes the duty of a disciplinary wife with calm and matronly enjoyment.

'THE GOVERNESS' 1993 SURVEY

OUR FIRST Membership Survey required the participation of Full (Lady) Members only, and was designed to uncover information about the attitudes and practices of the Disciplinary Female.

All Full Members were sent a Questionaire, which over 80 percent were kind enough to complete and return. Some of the results—published in Issue 4—were surprising, others less so.

LA CRÊME DE LA CRÊME

100% of Respondents considered that an interest in Discipline—from the Active or Passive point of view—was evidence of unusually high intelligence.

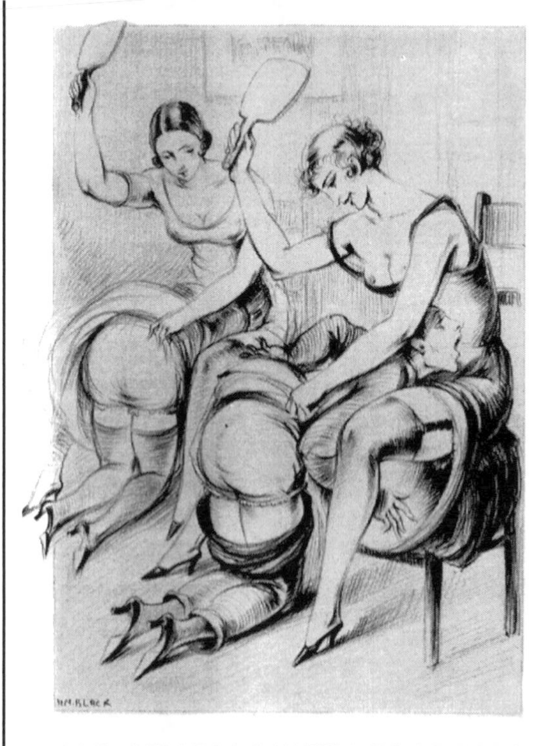

NO SEX BIAS WITH CULPRITS

Nearly sixty percent thought that females as well as males benefited from chastisement.

Males only: 41%.

FIRST CHOICE—OR LAST RESORT?

Forty-seven percent—a plurality—chose corporal punishment as a primary disciplinary option

41% said it would depend on their mood. Only 11% retained it as a last resort.

"GUIDE" READERSHIP LOWER THAN HOPED

Only 40% of respondents had read our Patroness's book *A Guide to the Correction of Young Gentlemen*.

60% had not, though half of this group planned to do so.

This was a very disappointing result.

"THE CORRECTION OF MISDEEDS" THE MAIN REASON FOR DISCIPLINE

Twenty-four of you cited this reason as the main stimulant of physical correction administered by yourselves.

18% each voted for "to heal the soul" and "to restore a balance".

13% apiece resorted to these measures "to restore domestic harmony" and for unashamed reasons of personal gratification.

6% used corporal punishment for its deterrent value.

These findings are of course by no means mutually exclusive.

SHOULD MALES WIELD THE ROD?

Seventy percent approve of men being allowed to employ physical discipline (upon both sexes). For 30% of them specific female sanction would be a further requirement.

Thirty percent of you thought that men should *never* wield the rod.

FEMININE PERCEPTIONS OF THE MALE CULPRIT

A surprising twenty-six percent perceived (and dealt with) any males under their jurisdiction as Slaves.

Nearly as large a percentage—22%—saw theirs as a quasi-parental rôle.

Eighteen percent (each) saw males as juveniles—schoolboys or delinquents or both—while a mere fourteen percent (again, a surprising figure) chose to obtain the benefits of domestic service from those who they disciplined.

JIM. BLACK

PUNISHMENT SHOULD BE PRIMARILY PAINFUL

Fifty percent of Respondents felt that the chief purpose of corporal discipline is the infliction of measured physical pain.

Twenty-eight percent thought that the inculcation of Shame was the major objective.

Only 11% thought that erotic stimulation should be a primary purpose.

PUNISHMENT SHOULD BE INFLICTED IN A CALM SPIRIT

For forty percent of Respondents all discipline should be administered calmly and without haste.

27% of you also believed that Ritual has an important part to play.

Less than five percent of you favoured instant, summary correction.

18% said it would depend on circumstances.

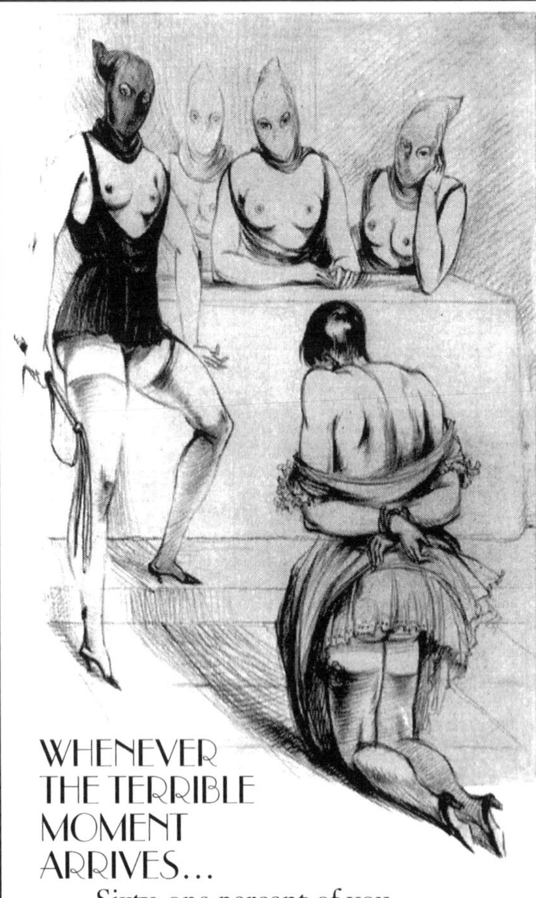

WHENEVER THE TERRIBLE MOMENT ARRIVES…

Sixty-one percent of you announce a punishment, then proceed to administer it without delay.

Thirty-three percent favour deferring the administration of an announced award until a later time.

A tiny percentage is prepared to inflict a punishment without notice or warning of any kind.

FIRST CHOICE OF WEAPON: THE SCHOOL CANE

Twenty-seven percent of you opted for the classic classroom instrument as their first choice of punishing tool.

18% favoured a riding-crop.

The Birch-rod, Strap, Paddle, Hairbrush and bare Hand each scored the modest mark of eleven percent. The Martinet, Switch, Slipper and Wooden Spoon received no marks.

SECOND CHOICE: THE STRAP

This was a close event, with a wide range of preferences. Thirteen percent favoured the Strap (if their first choice was not available).

11% would reach for either a Crop or a Birch-rod as their second choice of ferrule

The Martinet, Switch, Paddle and bare Hand all scored ten percent each. Hairbrush and Wooden Spoon attracted a mere seven percent apiece, while the lowly Slipper could only manage five percent.

QUI VA DÉCULOTTER?

Forty-one percent of you preferred to do your own stripping.

35% consider that this task is the culprit's duty.

To our surprise, 24% might consider employing the services of a trained assistant for this intimate and intimidatory purpose.

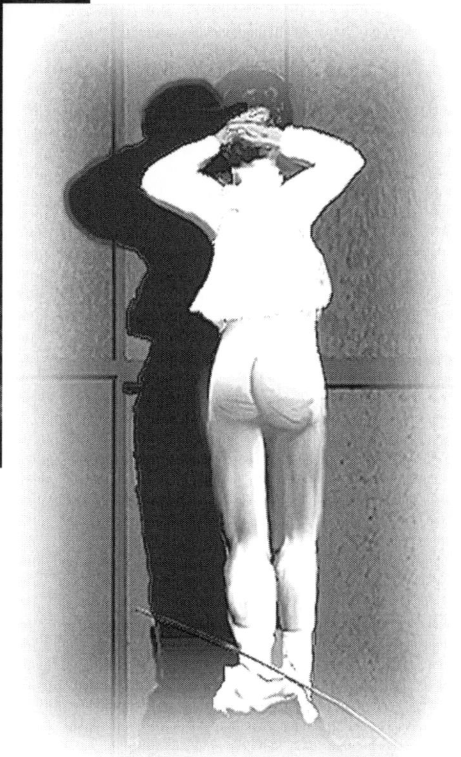

"STAND IN THE CORNER"

This traditional penalty is favoured by fourteen percent of Respondents as an "auxiliary" punishment.

Scolding and confiscation of clothing achieved 11 percent each.

Washing out the mouth, sending to bed, confinement, extra duties and impositions each scored 9%.

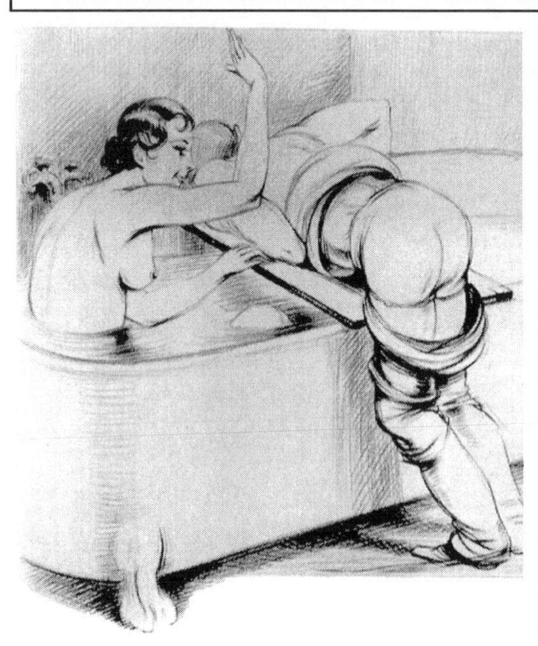

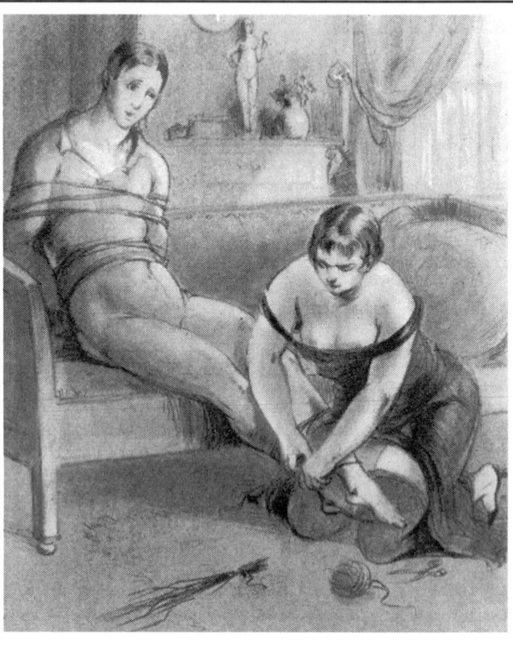

BARE BOTTOMS

This was one of only two questions on which the response from participating Respondents was unanimous. One hundred percent believed in baring the culprit's bottom as a matter of routine.

USING RESTRAINTS

No less than seventy percent had used restraints of some kind as part of a physical punishment, and would be willing to do so again.

WHEN SHOULD LINES BE WRITTEN?

Fifty-eight percent of Respondents considered that punitive impositions should be written out in advance of any further (i.e. corporal) punishment.
42% preferred to defer this stage until later.

THE GLARE OF PUBLICITY

50% were willing to administer corporal punishment in public "in serious cases", 17% "at any time", 29% never.

MOST SEVERE WEAPON: THE CANE

Responding Governesses were asked to range five well-known implements in perceived order of severity. The results were: Cane 74%; Birch 72%; Strap 72%, Hairbrush 44% and Palm 36%.

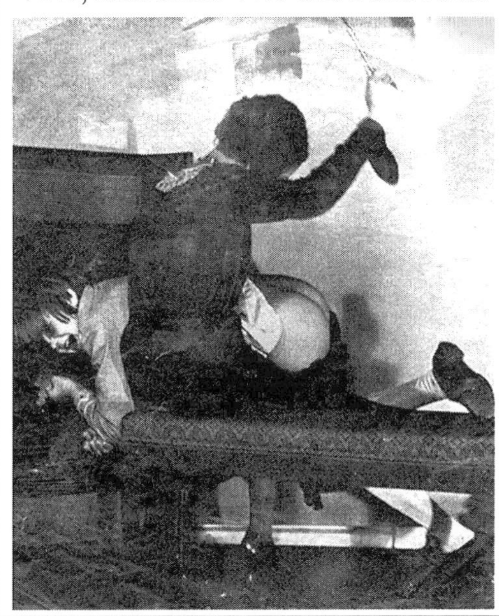

NO REMISSION

A large majority (64%) had a policy of continuing with a physical punishment until the moment of its pre-ordained ending. 28% might remit some strokes if and when tears make an appearance. A tiny percentage (0.5%) continue until weariness supervenes.

In Praise of NATURAL OBJECTS

JACQUELINE OPHIR

THE OTHER DAY I was glancing through one of the multitudinous—and to my mind rather dreary—magazines with which our own *Governess* is sometimes compared. Not so much of a magazine, more a catalogue, I said to myself, turning its pages and noticing the remarkable number of advertisers offering for sale purpose built chastisement impedimenta, including instruments of all types. And I was struck, not for the first time, but more sharply than ever before, by the innate vulgarity of many of these soi-disant tools of the dominant's craft.

Since I am about to give voice to a prejudice, let me say at once that of course like all prejudices it is unsustainable in serious debate, not least because at bottom these matters are always highly subjective. I do not seek to dictate others' views. Nevertheless, as an Englishwoman (not as proud to be so as once I was but still proud nonetheless) I fancy I detect a certain Transatlantic, or perhaps I should say Disneyish flavour in the rather obsessional design variance that afflicts many of the instruments now available. Straps of this or that grade of leather (or rubber), in a multitude of lengths and widths, embossed or mounted with handles, with no tails, two tails, three tails or a veritable forest of tailettes. Crops of different lengths and grades of flexibility, with or without "keepers", finished with cord, with leather, with rubber, with plain wood; handled with wood, with rubber, with leather, with cord or even with silver—the silver etched, if you wish, with the design or motif of your choice. And Paddles! Was there ever such a universe of tapette design? Rectangles, ovals, circles, irregular shapes, with all the variances of mounting, materials, flexibility, weight, colour, size, length, width and finish that are to be found with the straps and the crops. Martinets? Not so much variance here—chiefly in the number and length of the tails; and there is not a great deal even Americans anxious to display technical prowess can do to a cane—though such as it is, they do it: with straight handles bound in soft cloth or felt, often gaily coloured...

For me, puritan that I am, this is somewhat to miss the point. What, after all, is the special nature of the magic that gives any instrument its particular potency? Is it the lovingly carved woodwork of its handle—or the associations with discipline and punishment that the weapon would convey even without the craftsmanship? Which image carries more of this true magic: the ornate rubber paddle brandished by the professional dominatrix—or the carefully selected but still rude (in the sense of being au naturel) hazel switch in the firm grasp of an adored but respected lady friend? I venture to suggest that for persons of refinement it will invariably be the latter—for the power and potency of any implement do not reside in their construction but in their function; and though in some cases design can improve function, it is not often so.

In addition, I believe that domestic discipline of the type espoused by this Society is, above all, a perfectly natural proceeding (that ought to be the model for society in general but alas! is not likely to be so in my lifetime). There is something rather calculated about instruments that have been manufactured by professional weapon-designers. The underlying implication behind a strap built to last for a half-century is that its owner expects to be whipping away just as busily in fifty years' time! And while for some of us this may indeed be a true prophecy, for me there remains always the possibility that the next whipping I administer may be the last ever. Circumstances may change; the culprit may reform beyond all recognition—anything may happen. And to "invest" in a costly (for they are often costly, these liturgies) weapon or item of furniture seems to me to be taking a good deal for granted; "pricing the unborn calf", as Moslems say, even a form of hubris. And—may I say it?—in questionable taste.

Instruments that I consider "natural" (therefore tasteful) and eminently practical (that is, useful) include the palm of my hand, the switch, and the birch-rod. However I enlarge the category to include instruments that nominally (or even primarily) serve another duty—the point being that these are not instruments designed expressly for use in corporal punishment, though as tradition reminds us they serve remarkably well in this capacity.

Where should we be without the hairbrush, the carpet slipper, even—at a pinch—the wooden spoon? In days gone by housewives would often use carpet-beaters, butter-paddles, spatulas, razor strops, even laundry beaters in order to discipline their families; but these instruments are no longer readily to be found, and in most modern households would stand out from the toasters, microwaves and dishwashers by their very elegance and antiquity.

There are exceptions: the indispensable rattan cane is a "natural" object, certainly (though "natural" to East Asia, where it grows, rather than the Western Hemisphere) and succeeds æsthetically. However, once formed into its traditional curve, it loses all chance of being passed off as something else and must be kept hidden away. I do not mean by this that I am anxious to pass off instruments of chastisement as other items because I am ashamed of the way I conduct my life, but because it is not always politic to "reveal all" (as Members will agree). There are those of one's acquaintance who Know All, so to speak, and a great many more who Know Nothing (and never shall). To leave canes, martinets and doubled-tailed straps lovingly tooled with woodshed scenes in high relief et al lying around one's house severely circumscribes one's ad hoc social life. But a hairbrush on the dining room table, say, while out of place, is not overly remarkable—though to a culprit "in the know" its appearance in such a location may convey unspoken messages that set his limbs a-tremble in ways that many of you will undoubtedly recognise! ✤

A SCIENTIFIC BASIS FOR

The *Forschungsinstitut Für Körperlichebezuchtigung* was founded in 1919 following allegations of declining standards of corporal punishment in State reformatories[1]. Under its Director, Frau Doktor Gesäßjäger, the *Forschungsinstitut* published many scientific papers, in the first instance to encourage sound practice in corrective whipping, but later, when more advanced technology became available, to study mechanisms of punitive pain generation.

The following summary paper, intended for a lay audience, was presented by the Director as the Introductory Address to the 1924 *Konferenz aus Disziplin* organised by the Ladies Committee of the Swiss Lutheran Church Assembly[2]. The Conference was attended by English speaking delegates, for whom a translation was provided by the organisers. In spite of some imperfections, that translation has been preferred for reproduction here, because of the authentic flavour it provides.

DEAR LADIES! In meeting here we are united in our noble aim, to make from our young people good citizens for the new world, through the wonderful habit of strong discipline. God has told us to love our children with the rod[3], but do we do it good enough? Some years ago I was privileged to begin my study of these matters, and what a pretty mess I found! I am happy to tell you now I have tightened this looseness, and I will relate to you today some of the principles and details[4] we now use to make God's correction the most feared and therefore the best way of discipline that we know. By listening carefully, dear ladies, all who bring rods to naughty bottoms, you too will learn something about its up-to-now undiscovered possibilities, and I hope you will be inspired to go back to your homes, nurseries, schools and hospitals, everywhere God gives you the opportunity, to try for yourselves these good methods, and bring the wonderfull gift of stern discipline to all who must have it. And you know, that means every child in the land, from the babies to the big ones, none shall escape it. *[Applause]*

Corporal punishment must be correctly on the buttocks with various types of beaters, so our first task is to make better the canes, leather straps and birch bunches, those good friends what we know from old times, by their size, weight, fine manufacture, and so on. In the beginning days we had not measured their effects scientifically so we did ask judgements from our very well experienced *Zuchtmeisterin*, all of course are women, you will like to know.

TEST PROGRAMME

THE FIRST testing programmes, like the rest, was made with juvenile delinquents as subjects, as part of their treatment each day in the youth reformation school[5]. In Table 1

1. *Zuchthäuse.* 2. *Zuchtmeisterin.* 3. *Ruteleben.* 4. Methods 5. *Jugendszuchthaus.*

CORPORAL PUNISHMENT

Forschungsinstitut für Körperlichezüchtigung

1905 Begründet

Zeitschrifte Winter 1912

Sonderausgabe zur
Konferenz aus Disziplin

"Die Wissenschaft von Körperlichezüchtigung"

Frau Doktor H. Gesäßjäger,
Direktor, FFK

Post/Telegraph: FFK, Reuestraße 99, Birkegarten, Zürich

we see the results of simple tests for the standard birch rod.

To explain a little the results we see the pain we make by a single stroke of good birch, and the time for this pain to go down to one-half. The boys and girls are not telling us directly these numbers, we estimate them from the crying noise, bei the calibrated mikrophon, and how they are jumping after one good stroke, measuring by the strumming[6] in the holding straps[7].

We see at once the problem that the punishment is different for all, even when the

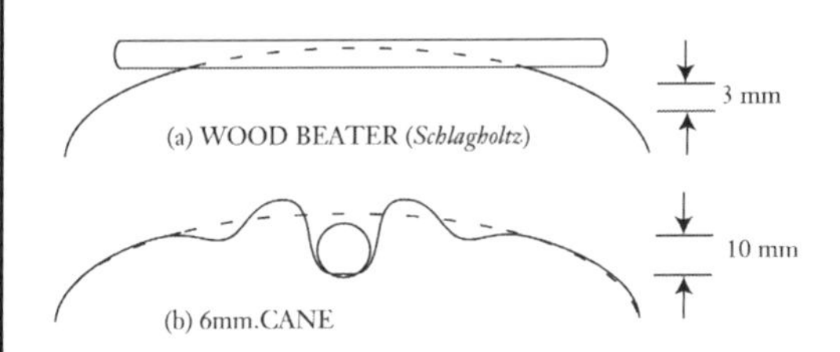

FIG.1: BUTTOCKS DEFORMATION by BROAD BEATER (a) and 6mmCANE (b)

Zuchtmeisterin tries so diligently in giving equal hardness in all cases, she is very correct in these things. And always the boys are making more difficulties[8] than the girls, sometimes we need three or four persons to help them be ready to say "Hallo" to our good birches, but I am happy we never allowed even such strong youths to go away from our nice medicine! Because of the variability, our Mathematiker, Fraulein Herzlos, is asking on very much whipping, more than 500 samples for good statistics, when we measure our different beaters, like the flexible canes, stiff paddle[9], leather straps, and so wider[10]. In Table 2 are results for all these good beaters[11], like the ones you are swinging[12] in your own houses.

I must say it, it can be hard for you to bring such nice punishment in your own houses when you must ask your mischievous culprits "Please lie still for the rod reception", because you have not comfortable beds[13] like we are using in the Jugendhaus, which hold fast the naughty ones, so they must not say "No thank you Mother, your discipline I don't need it today". Bei the Forschungsinstitut we are

6. Gyrating 7. Attached to the whipping bench 8. *Anstrengung* 9. *Schlagholtz*
10. Trans. *und so weiter* "and so on". 11. *Schlager.* 12. *Stockschwinge* 13. Benches

making designs for all such things like that, so strong couches, as well as the excellent beaters, and so on, then all families shall buy what the children need so anxiously.

We try to keep the weight of these beaters the same as far as possible, and ask the wardress to hit the buttocks only so strong like an ordinary mother or teacher would do it. You see how all give splendid correction, with some special qualities for springy cane[14], which cuts well and gives good feeling for many hours, even with only five strokes. These birches, like you can make at home from the trees, give excellent agony[15], which is going quickly away and so you may do it again on the backside, and again, so many times in each hour, and all the days, it's the best thing I think.

In the last word, I hear you say "But Frau Direktor, we knew already these things, this birches sting very good, a trembling cane[16] works good for two days, maybe three, in the bottoms". If so, dear Ladies, you are correct, and so perhaps it was not necessary in the end that our staff ladies[17] are giving so many lashes to find this out. Never mind, I am sure our boys and girls are happy to help us in this way! *[Laughter]*

ADVANCED TECHNIK

AFTER THE first research we try to understand better the different pains and how we start them in the best way. First we measure it better with the electric waves coming from the nerves in the bottom, with small skin electrodes. So you find a little jump when the birch comes softly, then a bigger one when it comes properly. Next we must use the calibrated whipping maschinen that we have made thanks to our excellent Ing. Festzubinden. The third one (special tool) is

***FIG.2:** BEATER DENSITY and VELOCITY for DIFFERENT PAIN LEVELS*

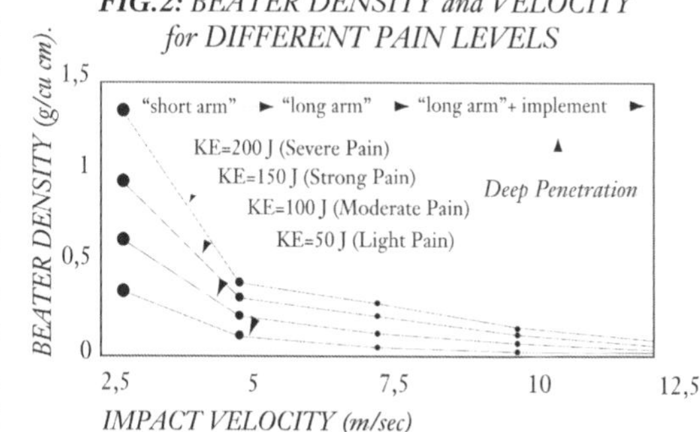

IMPACT VELOCITY (m/sec)
Impact velocities are typical for implement radii shown (striker distance from donor shoulder)

the Blitzlichtphotographmaschin[18]. By all these Apparaten we are proving how good is the theory[19] that we ourselves are the first Laboratorie to develop.

When the light-in-weight-rod going so fast meets the soft cushion, what is called the buttock, it stops only when it has gone "inside" a little distance, like Fig. 1. Our photos shows us sometimes this distance "d" as much as 2 or 3 centimetres for the round cane, but you don't see it without the photo, so quick it is. From this distance "d", and the density of the rod (that means how heavy), and its as well speed, and the density of the bottom (fat or lean), we find the average force of the rod after impact, from this formula,

$$\text{Force } F.d = \text{Konstant}.g.m.v^2$$
(g = *acceleration due to gravity*)

For a 50 gram cane, the hitting weight m.g is maybe only 5 gram, then for v = 25 m / sec, d = 10 mm, the force F = 104 kg! That is a rather large force from such little cane, but only the average, so the maximum will be much higher (so high I don't tell you!).

Some more measurements told that this maximum force controls the pain intensity, and the penetration "d" tells how many hours

14. *Rohrstock* 15. *Qualfoll.* 16. *Bewegungsfreirohrstock*
17. *.Zuchtigungsrechtsmädchen* 18. High speed camera 19. *Korperlichezuchtigungtheorie*

they feel it in the bottom. So we can change all such things by the velocity, density, and so on, to make pain levels in different ways, as shown in Fig 2.

From this already we learn basic principle of rod-technology, but yet we must consider the size of the "footprint", that is the beaten area for each stroke, for this controls the local pressure, that we know works directly on the bottom nerves.

Local pressure P = F / beaten area A

Look back at Fig 1 to see how the area A is different in the two examples, first the Schlagholtz so big, with small penetration, and then the cane with a thin stripe only, and deep penetration. If the force F is the same, then P is much smaller for the big Schlagholtz. But our first equation tells that the small penetration "d" of the Schlagholtz makes much higher the force F! And so the flat beater can be more hurtingful[20] than the thin cane that cuts so well in (but his pain is more quickly over)!

So this tells all beaters what we know are good, they are making all the same pain when the mass m and the velocity v are enough, but naturally they have a different taste for the boys and girls. So for this we can give something nice for the children, green birch at breakfast for example, then for lunch this bending cane, and then are coming the smooth leather straps for the supper, they enjoy such variety I think.

But now comes the most hard problem, to make uniform the pressure P over the footprint. In Fig 1 we see all swung beaters are having higher velocity at the outer end, so are hurting most in that part. When they are flexible, like the whip, the most hurting place may be only this little point at the end of the lash. See too, if you strike wrong with the semi-stiff rods, like canes and birches, the end is flying over with very high speed, and in the wrong place. We never overcome this difficulty when the rod-end is flying in a circle, and for this we make our whipping maschinen so special, the beaters are coming down only in a straight line (how they come down!). But I think you ladies can make good pressure distribution with stiff beaters, or bending ones that are very long, hitting only with the last, end parts on the soft place.

Now, in the last, you will also ask me why this good pressure distribution, why not give them hot pains in little places? The answer, my dear friends, is Kontroll. The best discipline for our young people is a long-time kind, one hour or so on the whipping bed, and we do that only when the pains level is correct—we don't wish after all to be unkind to our dear young ones, isn't it true? *[Laughter].*

And such wishes remain our aim for the future, with our new approaches to this marvellous research, based on dynamic analysis of *Hinterteilschockwelle*[21], and their stimulation of *Subkutannervenstechen*[22]. With such Technik can one see how is the vibration touching the nerves under the skin, and, you will be surprised, if you see our high-speed pictures, what *Erdbeben*[23] is moving in the first moments after one good stroke with the cane. And from such things our experts design already new kinds of instruments, like you never saw before, to better find these sensitive nerves in our bottoms. Perhaps one day, dear Ladies, you will ask me here again so that I can tell you something about such exciting new work. Until that day, I know you will not relax your good disciplines, and I greet to all and every one of you, "Heil, alle Guten Zuchtmeisterin".

[Rapturous applause]

20. *Peinlich* 21. Shock waves in the buttocks 22. Subcutaneous nerve endings. 23. Earth tremors